"You're *not* the man I remember," Ari murmured

Mark grinned. "That poor bastard you were engaged to was too staid, too conventional, too suffocating."

"Whereas you wouldn't hesitate to seduce me?"

"Dangerous words," he said. The firelight played across his face. "I take that as a challenge."

Then he kissed her. It was a tender kiss at first, but then it grew more passionate. Mark reached between them, loosening the tie of her robe so he could caress her body. His tongue probed her mouth.

Digging her fingers into his hair, she pulled his face back to see his eyes. "Didn't it occur to you this might not be a good idea?" she breathed.

"The thought went through my mind," he replied hoarsely. "But I didn't dwell on it for long."

With that he teased each corner of her mouth. Then before she could say a word, he kissed each breast, tautening her nipples. Ari moaned, closing her eyes as his lips trailed slowly downward and across her abdomen. The feel of his mouth nearly drove her over the edge.

In a haze, Ari realized Mark was having the wedding night she'd denied him—and herself. But ulterior motives didn't matter. Nothing did, except the exquisite sensation of his lovemaking....

Dear Reader,

At one time or another, most of us wonder what the future will hold—romance or mystery; fame or fortune; heartache or bliss. Some of us read our daily horoscope, others wait to see what will happen. I love fortune cookies. At best, there's a promise of something wonderful down the road. At worst, I get to eat a terrific cookie!

Fortune cookies are the premise behind the anthology *Fortune Cookie* (September '97). I hope you enjoyed my particular story, "Double Trouble." Attorney Zara Hamilton gets more than she bargained for when she switches places with her identical twin. On the adventure of her life, Zara is chased by criminals, but is rescued by a sexy ex-cop and finds romance.

The fortune cookie premise continues in my Superromance novel, *This Child Is Mine* (October '97). Zara's client Lina Prescott goes to a fertility clinic, where she receives a fertilized egg. It turns out the egg was stolen, and sexy Webb Harper, the father of her unborn baby, wants his child.

Lastly, in *Double Take* we meet Zara's twin, Arianna, who runs into ex-fiancé Mark Lindsay. Sexy, dangerous, *fun*, he's no longer the dull banker she left at the altar. And his mission is to rescue Arianna from herself!

I hope you enjoy all these books. And the next time you open a fortune cookie, may your fondest wish come **true**!

Sincerely,

Janice Kaiser

Janice Kaiser
DOUBLE TAKE

Harlequin Books

TORONTO • NEW YORK • LONDON
AMSTERDAM • PARIS • SYDNEY • HAMBURG
STOCKHOLM • ATHENS • TOKYO • MILAN
MADRID • WARSAW • BUDAPEST • AUCKLAND

For Birgit Davis-Todd, who went
above and beyond the call of duty on this one.
Thanks!

ISBN 0-373-25759-7

DOUBLE TAKE

Copyright © 1997 by Belles Lettres, Inc.

This edition published by arrangement with Harlequin Books S.A.

® and TM are trademarks of the publisher. Trademarks indicated with
® are registered in the United States Patent and Trademark Office, the
Canadian Trade Marks Office and in other countries.

Printed in U.S.A.

_____Prologue_____

SHE PACED back and forth across the tiny front room of her apartment, first pulling the ring from her finger, then jamming it back on. Arianna Hamilton glanced down at her left hand every once in a while, then bit her lip. Her engagement ring was the most beautiful thing she'd ever seen—a three-carat emerald-cut diamond set in platinum. When Mark had given it to her on Valentine's Day, she thought she'd die of happiness.

Taking the ring off again, she clenched it in her fist and went to the window. As she gazed down at the leafy tranquillity of Murray Hill at dusk, Arianna thought about the elegant town house Mark had bought for their future home. Recalling their plans to fill it with the kind of antiques they both loved, she felt like crying. It seemed impossible that she would consider giving up that dream—yet that was exactly what had happened. No matter how much she loved Mark Lindsay, she'd come to realize she couldn't marry him.

The phone rang just then and she was glad. It would be her twin sister in Aspen, returning her call. She snatched up the receiver.

"Hello? Zara?"

"No, darling, it's me." It was Mark. "Just wanted to let you know I'm running late. Board meeting ran over and now I'm stuck in traffic on Lexington Avenue. But I shouldn't be too long. Say, fifteen or twenty minutes."

"Uh, that's fine, Mark. I haven't started dinner. I can put things on at any time."

"Well, don't rush. I've got a bottle of Cristal with me. I thought maybe we should celebrate the fact that the wedding's only a month away."

"Oh, Mark," she murmured as tears bubbled from her eyes.

"I know I'm a sentimental fool, but I love you. Besides, I just can't help myself."

Arianna bit her lip so hard she almost broke the skin.

"See you soon," she mumbled. She hung up the phone and wiped the tears from her cheeks with the back of her hand. How on earth would she find the right words to tell him?

She walked aimlessly through the apartment. Winding up in her bedroom, she opened the closet and stared at the clear plastic clothes bag that protected her wedding gown. Instantly, Arianna recalled the day she'd found the dress. She had been shopping for weeks, searching high and low for that one perfect gown. Being petite, the last thing she wanted was a huge skirt, or a train that went on forever, or big floppy bows. She had nearly given up hope of ever finding her dream dress when she'd spotted a simple bias-cut gown in the window of a small bridal boutique.

She had rushed into the shop, practically undressing on the way to a fitting room. Even before the smooth satin slid over her hips, Arianna had been certain it was *the* one. A thousand times since, she had pictured herself walking down the aisle in that dress. She'd visualized the expression of Mark's face when he first saw her. And now, knowing she'd never ever wear it, Arianna was sick at heart.

Pangs of uncertainty shot through her. Was she being an idiot? A fool? On paper, Mark Lindsay was the perfect catch. He was good-looking, his credentials and qualifications impeccable. He was from a socially prominent family, and someday the investment banking firm of Lindsay and Soames would be his. Far more important, she had known right from the start that Mark truly wanted her. He was loving and attentive, a terrific lover. She'd never once doubted the depth of his feelings or his sincerity. But...

It was the "but" that bothered her. It was so hard to put her finger on what was wrong. Mark was probably every woman's dream man. Yet instead of reveling in his attention, Arianna often felt...she wasn't sure...maybe smothered by it.

The telephone rang again. This had to be Zara. Arianna picked up the phone.

"A matter of life and death, huh?" her sister said. "I canceled a settlement conference to make this call. It'd better be good, Ari."

"Zara," she said, her voice shaking, "I'm calling off the wedding."

"You're *what?*"

"I'm calling off the—"

"I heard you, Arianna. The question is *why?* What's happened?"

"Nothing's happened. It just doesn't feel right."

"But you seemed so certain before. Mark was perfect in every way."

"Maybe that's the problem. I know it doesn't make sense, but sometimes I think he's too solicitous, too dependable, too steady. All he wants is to make me happy."

"God, that *is* rough," Zara said sardonically.

"I know I sound like a raving lunatic. I often wake up in the middle of the night and wonder if I'm losing my mind. But then I tell myself these kinds of doubts aren't natural. My subconscious is trying to tell me something."

"Have you discussed this with Mark?"

"I've hinted around, but he's so sweet, so concerned about me, that he doesn't see my feelings for what they are. He's coming over tonight. Tomorrow we were planning on going to Martha's Vineyard to spend Labor Day weekend at his family's summer home. But I'm not going." She took a deep breath. "Zara," she said, her voice shaking, "I'm going to give the ring back tonight."

There was a pause before Zara replied. "You're sure? Absolutely sure? This isn't some sort of panic attack, is it?"

"No. It's been building for months. I think about it constantly."

"Was there some incident? Did you have a fight?"

"No, Mark's never raised his voice with me once. Sometimes I wish he would."

There was another silence on the line. This one lasted for several moments. Arianna could feel her heart pounding. She felt as if she were about to explode.

Zara finally spoke. "You always did like men with

an edge, a bastard with a good heart. I do understand when you say Mark's too nice."

"Then you don't think I'm crazy?"

"Sure, you're crazy, Ari, but that's not news."

Arianna laughed, somehow feeling better. Though identical twins, in many ways they were mirror opposites. Zara, a lawyer, lived in Aspen and had a small-town outlook on life, while Arianna, who edited celebrity biographies, loved the lights and glamour of New York City.

For the most part, the twins enjoyed the fact that they had different life-styles and needs. The downside was they didn't get to see each other often enough. That was extra important since their paternal grandmother had died two years earlier. Ellen Hamilton had raised them in Denver after their parents died in a plane crash shortly before their tenth birthdays.

"You're aware that last-minute cancellations inconvenience a lot of people," Zara said.

"Yes," Arianna replied. "And I can't tell you how badly I feel about that. You and Darcy and Laura have bought your bridesmaids' dresses. And Laura has her ticket to New York."

"I do, too," Zara said. "But I can come anyway, unless you'd rather I didn't."

"No, I'd love to see you. In fact, I can't think of anything that would mean more to me right now. Since you and Laura both have your tickets, maybe the four of us can make a reunion of it. The bridesmaids' dresses are a loss, I know, and I'm sick about that, but the trip doesn't have to be."

"You're right. Besides, we haven't gotten together

nearly as often as we promised ourselves we would after high school."

"Good. We can all go to Madame Wu's Destiny House one night. I don't think I've told you about it, but the place is really special. The fortune cookies are magical. They come true!"

"Arianna, you *have* flipped out."

"No. It really is a neat place, Zar. I'm sure you'd get a kick out of it." She paused and when she spoke again there was a catch in her voice. "But we don't have to go if you don't want to. Mainly, I'm trying to find ways to make it up to you guys for all the trouble I've created."

"Well, don't lose any sleep over us," Zara said. "We'll survive. You've got Mark to worry about now."

"Yes," Arianna said with a shiver. "And it's killing me."

"You'll get through this, Ari. You've never run from hard decisions in the past. And whatever you wind up doing, I'll support you one hundred percent. I think you know that."

"Thanks. That means so much," Arianna said. "You're the only one I can talk to about things like this. We've really only got each other."

"Ah, yes," Zara said with a sigh. "How well I know. Mother, daughter and sister all at once."

"Thanks for being there for me," Arianna said.

"Love you, sis. And don't suffer too much. Things will work out for the best. They always do."

"See you in a few weeks, then," Arianna said.

"Call whenever you need to talk."

She hung up the phone. Tears were running down her cheeks, but in an odd way, she was at peace. Zara had helped her to see that she was being herself, and that she was on track. Even though Zara was a small-town girl at heart, and didn't truly understand Arianna's world, she understood *her*. And right now, that was the biggest comfort of all.

1

MARK LINDSAY HAD DRIVEN the rental car up the twisting highway that led to Independence Pass, finally reaching the summit. Pulling over to the shoulder, he looked out at the bright snowfields sloping gently toward Mount Elbert to the north and La Plata Peak to the south. It was early in the season—only the beginning of October—but all that snow was an awesome sight, especially considering that he'd been in the Caribbean only thirty-six hours earlier.

Life had been one long series of emotional ups and downs for the last month. He'd felt torn when he left New York on the last day of September—on what would have been his and Arianna's wedding day—but he had flown to Martinique anyway, determined to find out if Arianna truly wanted to walk away from everything they had shared.

Though he hadn't been certain what kind of reception he'd get, he would never have guessed that he'd find himself in the Colorado Rockies three days later. Even more startling, both the stakes and the issues had changed dramatically. He still loved Arianna, but now he had to worry about her safety as well as her feelings.

Mark lowered his window to get a breath of the alpine air and take in the majesty of the vista. Despite the intense sunshine, at twelve thousand feet the thin air was never warm. He inhaled deeply, amazed at what fate had already taught him, even though he still hadn't caught up with Arianna.

Regardless of how this turned out, he'd discovered his mistake—he hadn't been true to himself. In his attempt to be good, decent and loving, he'd been dishonest without intending it. Most amazing of all, the realization had come as a complete surprise, which only went to show how blind he'd been. Though ego might have had something to do with it, as well, because he'd been totally blindsided the night she had broken their engagement.

"It's not that I don't love you, Mark," she'd said as she gave back his ring. "But I..."

"But you what?"

"I don't know. I guess I'm not ready."

"Not ready," he said, repeating her words. "Seven months isn't the longest engagement in the world, I grant you, but—"

"Mark," she'd said, getting up from the dining table, "it isn't a question of time." They were in the tiny front room of her upper-floor apartment in a brownstone in Murray Hill. They'd been facing each other over a single flickering candle.

"But you just said you're not ready."

She walked to the window, her back to him as she stared out at the dusk and the lights of Manhattan. Mark would never forget that image—her petite body tense, stiff, her soft red curls shining in the candlelight, her narrow little waist and the smooth curve of her hips so...so provocative and dear. Yes, he would always remember how he loved her and how it hurt to hear her say she couldn't marry him.

"It's not you, Mark," she'd said. "It's where I am right now. I can't really explain this. It's just... supposed to feel different."

"It seems to me you either love me or you don't."

Arianna turned, her eyes glistening. "No, it's not that easy. It really isn't."

"All right then," he said, "we'll put it off until you feel comfortable."

She shook her head. "No, it's not fair to you to postpone things. Six months from now I might feel the same and what would we have gained?"

"I'm willing to take the chance," he told her. "If I could just walk away, what would that say about my feelings for you?"

Tears started running down her cheeks. "Maybe you deserve better. Someone who can truly appreciate you. No, not maybe. I *know* you do."

At first, he'd been in shock. Sure, his pride had been wounded, but it was more than that. He didn't understand what had gone wrong. So, for a couple of weeks he did nothing, thinking Arianna would come to her senses, that it was fear of taking such a big step, nervousness, that had motivated her to break things off. Then, when he didn't hear from her, he slowly began to realize that wasn't the reason.

Not surprisingly, he wasn't the only one who'd been shocked and confused by what Arianna had done.

"What's wrong with the girl?" his mother had said when he broke the news to his parents. "All those celebrities and movie stars she's been dealing with must have gone to her head."

"That's not the problem, Mother."

"Perhaps not, dear. I didn't mean to imply that Arianna's other than a lovely girl, but...well, you loved Meredith, too. In fact, if you want my opinion, Meredith was more your type. It is such a shame she died in that awful car accident."

His mother had been partial to Meredith Peyton, the woman he'd been engaged to ten years earlier, though, to her credit, Julia Lindsay had never mentioned Meredith once Arianna had come along. Still, there was little doubt that to Julia, Meredith stood for all the things that counted—breeding, family, social connections.

Mark didn't share his mother's cynicism about Arianna, or her work. Editing celebrity bios and other exposé type books at Pierpont Books did put her in touch with notable personalities, it was true, but as far as he was concerned it was a broadening experience. When you rubbed shoulders with the famous, the powerful and the wealthy, you couldn't help taking on an allure of your own. It was part of who she was.

But there was no getting around the fact that being rejected hurt. Losing Meredith had been all his fault— he had accepted the blame for that a long time ago and he'd done his damnedest to avoid making that same mistake with Arianna. Yet, despite his best efforts, he'd managed to screw up this relationship, as well. What he still wasn't sure of was if she meant it when she'd said, "You deserve better. Someone who can truly appreciate you," or if she'd simply been trying to soften the blow.

He'd decided to find out. So, the week before they were to have been married, he called her at work.

"Richard?" she said, picking up the phone.

"No, Arianna. It's me, Mark."

"Oh, Mark, I'm sorry," she'd said, sounding embarrassed. "I had two calls at the same time and I must have pushed the wrong button. Richard Gere's on the other line to confirm an appointment. Could you hold? I won't be long." She was away only a minute. "Sorry," she said, coming back on the line.

"I hope everything's okay in Hollywood," Mark said, struggling to keep the sarcasm out of his voice.

"Richard's thinking of writing a book and his agent wanted him to talk to me about the ins and outs. It's just routine."

Arianna's tone had been conciliatory, apologetic even, which surprised him. At that point she owed him nothing.

"The reason I'm calling," he told her, "is that the honeymoon trip to Martinique is all paid for and it's too late to get a refund. I was thinking of going myself, but a big project has come up unexpectedly. I thought you might like to have your ticket and the reservation at the Maison des Caraïbes."

"You're suggesting I take the trip, even though the wedding was called off?"

"It's paid for, Arianna. Why not take advantage of it?"

There was a silence on the line. Mark waited.

"You think I'm callous and insensitive, don't you?"

He was shocked by the anguish in her voice. "What?"

"You thought it was easy for me to break our engagement...as though it didn't matter."

"Arianna, I didn't mean to suggest—"

"Oh, it's not your fault. I suppose I can hardly blame you for thinking the worst."

"Look," he replied, "I was only trying to be thoughtful. We've got tickets and they're going to waste. I figured you might like to take advantage of yours, that's all."

There was another silence.

"I don't think I could," she said after a moment. "It was supposed to be our honeymoon...I mean...Lord, I *do* have feelings."

"Well, it's up to you. The ticket won't do me any good. I'll courier it and the hotel reservation over. Do as you wish with it."

That's the way the conversation had ended, and though he'd heard strong emotion in Arianna's voice, and she obviously felt guilty, there had been no sign that she might be reconsidering her decision.

Mark had been businesslike so as not to put any pressure on her, hoping that in opening the door he'd be giving her the opportunity she needed. But she didn't contact him. He knew then that if they were ever going to get together and talk, it would be up to him to take the initiative.

So the following Friday, the day before they were to have been married, he'd tried to reach Arianna at her office. To his chagrin, he'd learned from her assistant that she was out having dinner with Richard Gere. It was hard not to be jealous, though he knew he had no claim on her. Still, he had asked if Arianna would be in the office on Monday. It was then he discovered that she was going to Martinique, in spite of what she'd said.

That was all it took. Mark decided then and there to fly to the Caribbean, too. Their last conversation had convinced him that Arianna was suffering. That pained him because Meredith had also suffered, and he didn't want history to repeat itself—this time he would not be callous or cavalier. They would have a heart-to-heart talk and he'd do what he could to win her back. And if that wasn't in the cards, at least he'd be able to bring closure to their relationship.

Things hadn't worked out the way he'd planned. When he got to the hotel in Martinique, he found Arianna, all right, but she was with another man. At first he was outraged—God knew how hard he'd tried to do what she wanted, when she wanted it, and the thought that she'd been two-timing him burned him up. But as it turned out, he'd been mistaken. Ari hadn't come to Martinique. She'd gone to Aspen instead. It was Zara who had checked into the hotel, using her twin sister's reservation. And the man was a friend of Zara's.

Mark recalled Arianna telling him that the two had often switched places as kids, taking special delight in confusing and confounding their grandmother who'd had a terrible time telling them apart. They'd had similar fun in college, though Zara wasn't as keen on that kind of sport as Arianna by then. Which was why he'd been so surprised to find Zara in Martinique.

"She thought she could get some work done while

she deals with her heartache," Zara had explained to him in the lobby of the Maison des Caraïbes.

His interest had been piqued by the comment. "Real heartache, or are you just saying that to make me feel better?"

She gazed at him thoughtfully. "Don't tell her I said this, but Arianna isn't completely sure she did the right thing by calling off the wedding."

It was the best news he'd heard in a month. "She said that?"

"No, but I know Ari as well as I know myself," Zara answered. "We've always thought right along with each other, even when we reached different conclusions. I won't make any promises, Mark, but I will tell you this—my sister is still trying to decide how she feels about you."

"That's all I need to hear," he said. "I'm going to Aspen."

"Wait a minute," she said. "Not so fast."

"You think it's a bad idea?"

"No, it might even be a good idea. But if you're going, you ought to be prepared. The better you understand her feelings, the better off you'll be."

Mark shook his head. "Why didn't I talk to you a long time ago? Okay, shoot. Give it to me straight and don't worry about sparing my feelings."

"All right. You're a great guy, Mark, but I think you've been a little too nice," she told him. "Ari said you're the most caring, considerate, thoughtful man she's ever known, but, well, my sister's very independent." She paused, then said, "I think sometimes she felt a bit suffocated by you. I'm not suggesting she wants a man who acts indifferent to her, or anything like that. But if you want to get her to the altar, make her work for it. She needs someone who'll keep her on her toes, not cater to her every whim. Ari loves a challenge. If you keep that in mind, you'll have the key to her heart."

Zara's words had been a real eye-opener. He suddenly saw his relationship with Arianna in an entirely different light. Of course she felt smothered because smothering her was exactly what he'd done—he *had* catered to her every need, bent over backward not to offend, not to hurt or upset her. Ironically, in his struggle to avoid making the kind of mistake he'd made with Meredith, he'd done more harm than good. Worse, he had not been true to himself. He hadn't even been the man he really was.

It was more obvious than ever that Meredith's death on that icy road in Connecticut years ago—a terrible tragedy in its own right—continued to have an impact on his life. Not a soul knew he felt responsible for what happened, or that he'd carried the burden and the pain in his heart ever since. He had been much younger, of course, but he'd sworn never to let his selfishness and insensitivity hurt anyone again, especially not someone he loved.

And when Arianna had come into his life, he'd overreacted. He'd overwhelmed her with attention, not realizing he was addressing Meredith's needs and desires instead of Arianna's. Fortunately, Zara had helped him see what he'd done. He'd been both stupid and blind.

In spite of that realization, it bothered him that Arianna hadn't found a way to communicate her feelings. Had he been responsible for that, as well, or was it what he'd originally thought—that she didn't fully understand the problem herself? After all, how did a woman complain about being treated *too* well, about a man being *too* considerate? She couldn't, at least not easily. Yet he could see how painful her frustration must have been. Never had the expression "Nice guys finish last" seemed so apropos.

The bright side was that Zara had also given him an excuse to see Arianna again. After the twins had switched identities, a mobster who thought she was Arianna had handed Zara a sensitive manuscript at the airport in New York.

"It's a tell-all book that's got the Mafia in an uproar," she'd explained. "If you put it in Ari's hands, I won't have to worry." Zara had warned him there were risks. "There are people who'd kill to keep this from falling into the wrong hands. I mean *literally* kill. I'd almost rather Arianna didn't get it, but I also know she wouldn't want me making that decision for her. I'll leave it up to you to make sure she's all right."

That had put him on the horns of a dilemma. While he welcomed the excuse to see Arianna—and bring her something that would thrill her—giving her the manuscript also meant he would be subjecting her to danger. And if he tried to protect her, he'd run the risk of smothering her again. The challenge was to find a way to save her, and at the same time not lose her.

Zara had no suggestions. "I know it puts you in a tough situation," she'd said, "but I have a feeling this is something you need to handle yourself."

Zara was right about that, too. So he'd promised to keep Arianna safe. Then he'd taken the manuscript and grabbed the next plane to Miami, determined to be himself this time. If Arianna liked the sides of him she had never seen before—and probably hadn't even suspected he had—then somehow, someway, he believed things would work out. Unfortunately, that theory didn't tell him how to deal with the Mafia. If it came down to it, extraordinary measures might be required.

Mark took a last whiff of thin mountain air, checked the traffic, then pulled onto the highway. Aspen was less than an hour away and the woman he loved was waiting. She would be shocked to see him, but that would be nothing compared to the little surprise he had planned. Zara had insisted her sister wanted a man who kept her on her toes. Well, that was exactly what he intended to do.

ARIANNA ENTERED the shop on Mill Street where for the past few days she'd been picking up day-old copies of *The New York Times*. The proprietor took his pipe from between his teeth and nodded a greeting.

"Afternoon, Zara," he said. "Must be some extra New Yorkers in town because I had a run on the *Times*. But I saved you a copy."

"Thanks," she said with a grin as she took a five-dollar bill from her purse.

The man plopped the newspaper and her change on the counter. Arianna thanked him, then left the shop. She hadn't bothered to straighten him out as to who she was. After the first few attempts to explain to various townspeople that she was not Zara, but her twin, she found it easier simply to let them carry on with their assumptions.

Though she found the whole thing rather amusing, the night before they'd parted in New York, she had promised Zara there'd be no high jinks. "It might be fun to check out your boyfriends, I admit, but the last thing I'd want is to ruin your reputation," she'd said with a grin. "I know small towns are funny that way."

"I'm not worried about boyfriends, because at the moment I'm not seeing anyone," Zara had replied. "But I don't want to come home and discover I've been disbarred. Just don't be passing out legal advice!"

Arianna had laughed gleefully. "Oh, the possibilities!"

When she reached Main Street, Arianna turned west and strolled along in the pleasant autumn air, her newspaper under her arm. She enjoyed walking and had to be a little more careful in New York. Here she didn't have to think twice about it. So to take full advantage of the opportunity, she'd used Zara's car only once, when she'd gone to the supermarket. Mostly she'd stayed home, and with all the peace and quiet had gotten some work done, admittedly not as much as she'd hoped. Mark kept popping into her mind.

She'd be in the middle of reading a page when suddenly she'd picture the way he looked at the beginning of September, when they'd said goodbye for the last time. For a man who had just been handed back his engagement ring, Mark had been fairly stoic. Oh, his eyes had glistened and he had given her a sad smile, but he'd said something that about broke her heart. "The most important thing to me is that you're happy. If this is what it takes, then I guess this is the way it has to be. But it hasn't changed my love for you.''

Arianna checked her watch. In Martinique it was about dinnertime. If she hadn't broken up with him, they'd be together at that very moment, newlyweds, maybe sitting across from each other in the dining room. They would probably have made love a time or two already—once after a morning swim in the crystal-clear water of the Caribbean, and once while they were getting ready for dinner.

That would have been nice because Mark was wonderful in bed. She'd never known a more considerate lover, a man so sensitive to her every need. Yet even that, delicious as it was, could be a source of frustration. She would have liked it if every once in a while he'd swept her off her feet, had his way with her—not all the time, of course, but often enough to keep things interesting. Maybe that was the trouble, now that she thought about it. Perfect consideration could, after a while, become predictable and therefore boring.

Arianna had to laugh at herself. How many women would say she was nuts? After all, considerate lovers didn't grow on trees. Maybe she'd put too much emphasis on the importance of challenge and excitement. Nobody was perfect, and besides, what were the chances she'd find someone better?

But why was she torturing herself, thinking this way? She'd brought plenty of work with her. She should think about that, not what might have been. She'd given back the ring, now she had to live with the decision. Work had been her solace and it was to her work that she had to devote her energies. Still, she couldn't edit day and night. She needed some diversion. The trouble was, Aspen was almost too quiet in the fall. During the ski season it would be more lively, of course, but now the summer crowds were gone and the skiers hadn't yet arrived.

The only contact of consequence she'd had with anyone was that morning when Zara's friend, Lina Prescott, called the house.

"Gee," Lina had said when Arianna explained who she was, "your voice is just like Zara's."

Arianna laughed. "People say we look alike, too."

"I knew Zara was visiting her twin in New York, and I've seen pictures, but I didn't expect to be talking to you. She told me she'd be back by now."

"There was a change of plan," Arianna explained. "I had a trip to Martinique that was paid for and I couldn't go, so Zara went in my place. She'll be back in a couple of weeks."

"Oh dear."

There was worry in Lina's voice and Arianna asked her if something was wrong.

"Yes, something has come up and I badly need to talk to Zara. It's both a personal and legal problem."

"Why not call her? She's staying at the Maison des Caraïbes. I'm sure you can get the number from the operator in Martinique."

"Thanks," Lina said. "Maybe I will." Then she'd hung up.

Arianna had been thinking of calling Zara herself, but she didn't want to spoil her sister's vacation. Although her twin hadn't made a big deal of it, Arianna knew Zara had gone to the Caribbean hoping to find romance. She really hoped she succeeded.

Between them, Arianna had always had the more active social life. Zara tended to be the more serious twin and didn't do much casual dating. Arianna figured a fling would do her sister good, and the last thing she needed was her calling up to sob on her shoulder.

Taking the paper from under her arm, she glanced at the headlines as she strolled. When you were in the Rockies, all it took to remind you where the center of the world was located was to see a copy of *The New York Times*. One of the lead stories concerned the Middle East. Another was about congressional budget hearings. She was about to tuck the paper away when a story about a gangland slaying in the parking lot at John F. Kennedy Airport caught her eye.

Arianna skimmed the first few paragraphs, noting that a mobster by the name of Sal Corsi had been killed. There was no motive mentioned except for a reference to the fact that Corsi was thought to be on the outs with the leadership of the New York Mafia. What gave her pause was that the murder occurred at about the time Zara's flight had left for Miami.

She couldn't help wondering if the killing could have anything to do with Mr. X, the writer who had been pestering her to read his Mafia exposé. She had put the man off, promising to contact him after she returned from her vacation. But now she wondered if there was a connection between Corsi and Mr. X.

Reading about that sort of thing made her realize that New York could be exciting in more ways than one—not all of them good. There was something to be said for small-town life. Still, though she understood why Zara loved Aspen, it simply wasn't Arianna's cup of tea, not day in and day out.

She'd come to a cross street and was about to step off the curb when she heard a car brake. She glanced back to see it pull over just as someone called out to her.

"Hey, Zara, can I give you a lift?"

The voice was familiar. *Very* familiar. But she told herself it simply couldn't be. Could it? Bending down to peer through the window, she saw Mark. *Her* Mark! Well, the man who used to be her Mark, anyway. Arianna's mouth sagged open and she stared at him dumbly.

"My God," she said. "What are you doing here?"

He gave her a big grin. "I was driving through Colorado and thought, what the heck, why not drop by and say hello to my almost-but-not-quite, sister-in-law."

She blinked, wondering if he was putting her on. "Your what?"

"Come on, Zara, hop in!"

Arianna was still in shock. This, after all, was the man she was to have married only a few days ago. Could he truly believe she was *Zara*? Skeptical, she opened the car door and slid in. "Seriously, what are you doing here?"

"I cannot tell a lie," he said. "I came to see you."

"But why?"

He gave a shrug and sighed. "I thought maybe we could talk about Arianna."

She swallowed hard, concluding that he truly did think she was her sister. Of course, the honorable thing would be to set him straight before this went on too long. But before she could open her mouth, he put his hand on her knee and gave her that quirky smile of his, his soft brown eyes uncharacteristically mischievous.

"And while we're at it, maybe we can talk about you, too."

"Me?" she croaked.

He chuckled. "I think it ought to be clear that I'm attracted to your type."

"Mark!"

He gave her a wink. "Just kidding," he said. "But I do want to talk to you." He put the car in gear and proceeded down the street. "You'll have to direct me. I have your address, but I'm not sure where to turn."

"Two more blocks," she said numbly. "Then go right."

She glanced over at him, not believing what was happening. It had to be a joke, in spite of everything. But then, Mark was straight as a string. He would never trick her, which meant he really did think she was Zara.

Again she realized that the decent thing would be to tell him who she was before he embarrassed himself. But the devil in Arianna told her to wait and see what happened. That might not be fair, but mischief had always been her game. Unfortunately, Mark had never understood that about her—probably because he didn't have a mischievous bone in his body.

2

MARK PARKED in front of the Victorian house and turned off the engine. Arianna was embarrassed, yet strangely intrigued. True, she'd given her word that she would behave herself in Aspen—and not pretend to be Zara—but the *spirit* of her promise would not be broken because it hadn't been meant to include Mark. Besides, she figured this was too good to pass up.

"What did you want to talk about?" she asked.

"Arianna and I are through, I know that," he said. "But I need closure. I want to understand what happened between us so I can move on."

"Didn't Ari give you her reasons?" she asked, leading him on.

"Oh, she tried to explain, but she didn't do a very good job of it. To tell you the truth, I don't think she knew the reason herself."

Arianna's eyes flashed at the suggestion that she didn't know her own mind, but she kept her composure. "No doubt she was trying to be considerate. Arianna's really a very decent person, you know."

"Oh, yeah, she's decent," he said, rubbing his chin. "That's not her problem."

She squirmed, suddenly feeling guilty. Mark would just die if he knew who she really was, and she didn't want to be unkind to him. Not after what he'd gone through already. She should tell him who she was right now. But dammit, how often did a woman get a chance to hear the unvarnished truth...from a man?

"You obviously want to talk about it," she said sweetly. "Why don't we go inside and have a cup of coffee?"

"That'd be great," he said.

Mark grabbed a carry-on case from the back seat. They got out of the car and went up the walk.

"You have a nice little place here," he said. "I love small-town Victorians."

"You do?" she said with surprise. Unlocking the door, she glanced back at him. "Uh, Arianna told me you were a real city boy."

"Oh, I am," he said, "but there are a couple of sides to me. Actually, that's one thing about Arianna I didn't much care for. I don't think she ever really knew me. She has a tendency to see what she wants to see, you know."

"I don't think that's true at all!" she said tersely.

Mark arched his eyebrow and she knew she'd overplayed her hand. She would have to keep her emotions in check if she wanted to make the most of this situation. "I mean, I've never felt that about her. Ari can be intense, but she cares about people. I know she cared about you." She pushed the door open and went in the house.

"Well, you're right about her being intense. Arianna is very focused," he replied, following her to the living room. "So focused she sometimes doesn't see what's going on around her. What good does it do to care about someone if you're oblivious to who they really are or how they feel?''

His words stabbed deep into her heart, but she couldn't let her hurt show. "Do you *really* believe that, Mark, or are your wounded feelings talking?''

He smiled in an odd way before his expression turned solemn. "Arianna's a wonderful woman and a part of me will always love her. I'm sure that long after we've gone on with our lives, there will still be a place for her in my heart.''

A lump formed in Arianna's throat and her eyes welled with tears. She heard the tenderness in his voice and it was all she could do to keep from breaking down.

"But you've got to admit," he went on, "your sister can be a spoiled brat.''

Arianna blinked. "What?''

"She's pretty full of herself," he said.

Arianna grew bright red, but turned away so that Mark wouldn't see. "Don't you think that's a bit strong?'' she said, struggling to keep her voice even. "I've always found her mature and considerate.''

Mark sighed. "I don't mean to bad-mouth her, but I'm a little surprised by your reaction. Arianna told me herself that you once accused her of getting your share of the ego.''

She rocked back on her heels, forcing a smile. "Well, sisters say things like that from time to time. It doesn't mean I don't respect her." Then, clearing her throat, she said, "Sit down and make yourself at home. I'll put the kettle on.''

Arianna went off, grumbling to herself. She

shouldn't have gotten so upset. Of course he'd be bitter—she'd rejected him. And he thought he was talking to someone who'd be sympathetic.

As she put water on to boil, she started to wonder how Zara *would* have reacted. But before she came to any conclusions, she heard Mark enter the kitchen. She turned and saw him leaning against the door frame, his arms folded over his chest. He was looking her over, his expression more wry than she could ever recall seeing it. In fact, Mark did not at all seem himself. He let his eyes drift down her jeans-clad legs. "Need some help?" he said.

"No," she replied, feeling a bit flustered. "Thanks. I'm just going to put a couple of teaspoons of instant coffee in some mugs."

"Instant, huh? That seems more Arianna's style. I remember her telling me once that you were the old-fashioned one. You grind your own coffee, make your bread and preserves. Wasn't a lot of this stuff from your grandmother's kitchen?" he said, glancing around.

"Well, y-yes," she stammered, "but I ran out of ground coffee and I always keep a jar of instant for emergencies. If you'd rather not have any, I could—"

"No, no. Instant's fine. I was just a little surprised."

She nervously scooped some coffee crystals into the mugs, all the while feeling Mark's eyes on her. It was disconcerting, knowing he thought he was looking at her sister.

"You know," he said, "despite the fact that you and Arianna are identical, it still amazes me how much you two are alike physically. Right down to the smallest detail. And yet, as people, I know you're both very different."

"Yes," Ari said sardonically, "she's the evil twin."

Mark chuckled. "If I was harsh talking about her, I apologize. I know you love her, and she does have many good qualities." He moved closer to her and lowered his voice. "But I'm sure you have many of the same virtues, Zara."

Arianna gave him a double take. "Pardon?"

"I mean, I know there are differences between you and Arianna," he said, "but there've got to be similarities, too. The sort of qualities I found attractive in your sister."

Arianna gulped. Was Mark coming on to her? He certainly was studying her in a manner that was not at all like an almost-brother-in-law. A chill went through her. She backed against the counter.

"Mark, we've only met once. We don't know each other at all."

"True," he said with a smile. "But there's no reason we can't get better acquainted, is there?"

The bastard *was* flirting. Of all the nerve. "I thought you came here because you wanted to talk about Ari," she said as nonchalantly as she could.

"I did. But I'd be less than honest if I didn't tell you that you seem different than when we met last spring." His voice was a low growl. "Either that, or I'm seeing you through totally different eyes."

She blanched. "Different how?"

He thought for a moment. "Well, don't take this wrong, Zara, but you seem more like,...well, like Arianna."

She was relieved to hear that, but it was still disconcerting to think that the man she was to have married days ago was flirting with her sister. Just how broken up was he?

"Maybe *you're* seeing what you want to see," she said lightly.

"Or maybe I'm seeing someone with a lot of Arianna's good qualities, but at the same time isn't..." His voice trailed off.

"A spoiled brat?" she said, quoting him, her tone sharper than she intended.

He laughed and she went to the stove to check the water. He followed, coming right up behind her. She could feel the heat of his body and smell his cologne. Gucci...the one she'd given him for Valentine's Day.

"Sure I can't help?" he said.

"No, I can handle it," she said, giving him a glance over her shoulder.

He moved still closer.

"Hmm," he said. "Do you know you smell just like Arianna? That *is* Chanel, isn't it?"

"Yes...yes, it is."

When Mark took her by the shoulders and turned her around, she almost jumped. He grinned down at her. At five-ten, he was no giant, but he was still eight inches taller than she and he seemed very large and imposing. And this definitely wasn't a brotherly reaction she was getting from him.

"You know what?" he said, gazing into her eyes. "I've just made an amazing discovery."

Arianna was afraid to even ask.

"I'm very attracted to you."

She flinched. "Mark, no."

"What's wrong with that? It's a compliment."

"But don't you see, that's not good," she protested.

"Why not? It's true. You even smell like Ari."

"Well...what woman wants to be...liked...because she reminds a man of somebody else, even if it's her twin?" she said, unable to think of anything else.

Mark grinned. "Hey, I'm not that superficial. Don't you think I can see your special, unique qualities? I guess Arianna was just the starting point, but with you, Zara, I think things could be even better."

"Oh my God," she murmured.

He tightened his grip on her shoulders. Then, to her horror, he began to draw her toward him. Good Lord, was he was going to kiss her?

"Tell the truth," he murmured, "hasn't a part of you wondered if maybe *you* weren't the one who belonged with me?"

"No!"

"Really?"

"Mark, you aren't acting at all like yourself." She gulped, realizing that wasn't the way to phrase it. "Uh, what I mean is, this isn't the way Ari described you."

"Well, maybe she was so focused on herself that she didn't get to know the real me."

Arianna was dumbstruck. Was this really Mark Lindsay or did *he* have an identical twin she knew nothing about?

Before she was aware of what was happening, Mark kissed her. And not just a friendly kiss—it was full of passion. His lips moved over hers, nipping, teasing. He ran his hand down her back, cupping her waist and drawing her against him, just the way he used to do when he was kissing *her!* She felt herself starting to respond the way she always did, her heart beginning to lope. But then she remembered who *he* was and who he thought *she* was, and almost choked. Dammit, there was no way she could respond the way she used to. The way she wanted to now, if she were honest. Because Mark wasn't kissing *her*, he was kissing *Zara*. Or thought he was!

Wedging her hands between them, she managed to push him away. "This has gone on long enough!" she cried. "Can't you tell I'm not Zara? For God sakes, I'm Arianna!"

His response was a wide, thoroughly bemused grin.

"And I resent you trying to seduce me, thinking I was Zara! It's...it's..."

"It's what?"

"I don't know, like incest. I thought you were an honorable person, Mark Lindsay, but I'm beginning to realize I didn't know you at all!"

He threw back his head and laughed. Really laughed. After a minute, tears were coming from his eyes.

"You think this is funny?" she said, pushing past him and going to the table.

Mark took a minute to recover. "I knew it was you all along. I was just having a little fun," he said, turning to face her.

"You knew?"

"Yeah."

She was horrified. "How could you! I had no idea

you were this...mean...this inconsiderate. Really, Mark! This isn't like you."

He shrugged. "I know."

"I'm serious. Who were you before, if this is the real you?"

"That's the point I'm trying to make. I wasn't kidding when I said you were blind to a lot of things."

She felt really annoyed, yet she was uncertain whether her anger was appropriate. Maybe she should be hurt. Or embarrassed. It was hard to be sure.

"You can take consolation in one fact," he said. "I wasn't kissing Zara. I kissed you."

She glared. "Yeah. Well, how did you know who I was?"

"Zara told me you were here."

"I don't believe you. You got caught and you're trying to make the best of an embarrassing situation."

"No, it's the truth," he said.

She put her hands on her hips. Her expression was haughty. "If so, then I've got to tell you that what you did was dishonest. Ungentlemanly."

"Oh, yeah. Well, I didn't hear you stopping me to explain that you were really Arianna," he said, slowly walking toward her.

She squirmed uncomfortably. "Well...no...but that's different. *I* didn't set out to deceive you. And *you* did intend to deceive me."

"Come on, we were both having fun. I just happened to get the better of you this time." He stopped in front of her. Then, giving her a wink, he added, "The least you can do is admit it."

She chose to ignore that. "This is so unlike you," she complained.

"No, my dear, just unlike the man you thought you knew."

That got her dander up. "You aren't suggesting I almost married somebody I don't really know."

"Yes. But it's not entirely your fault," he replied, sighing. "I was determined to present an image and maintain it. I didn't do it with ill intent, but we fell into a pattern."

Arianna could see he meant what he was saying. Really meant it.

"I don't know what to say," she admitted.

"You know," he said, his eyes sparkling, "I haven't had many opportunities to see you this way."

She looked rueful. "You mean, feeling like a fool?"

"Oh, come on," he said, touching the ends of her hair. "It's not that big a deal. You're just not used to me having a little fun at your expense."

She shivered involuntarily. "Mark, you are not the man I knew."

He brushed her cheek with the back of his fingers. Arianna swallowed hard. Even his touch seemed different. It created all kinds of unexpected sensations. For heaven's sake, what was happening to her? This was the man she could have married but chose not to, the man who was so thoughtful and considerate she got bored.

"Maybe it has something to do with love being blind," he said, staring at her mouth. His hand moved up her arm and Arianna trembled. "Before, I think we were both deluding ourselves," he went on. "But now, who knows. Without the burden of marriage hanging over us, we might even be friends—better friends than before."

"M-Mark," she stammered, "this isn't fair."

"What isn't fair?"

The answer was "being so seductive," but how could she say *that* to him? He might think she actually liked this...which might be true on a superficial level, but not deep down.

"Arianna?"

The kettle began to sing, breaking the spell. "Excuse me," she said, slipping under his arm and returning to the stove. She filled the coffee mugs while Mark sat at Zara's tidy little table, the one she'd gotten from their grandmother. Arianna carried over the steaming mugs and handed one to Mark. Then she sat down, too.

Having gathered herself, she assumed a businesslike tone. "You honestly believe we were deluding ourselves? Until today, I would have said we knew each other fairly well."

"Things are not always as they appear," he said, taking a sip from his mug.

"Then perhaps it was for the best." She smiled tentatively. "Is that why you came, then, to prove to yourself we did the right thing?"

"No, actually, Zara wanted me to give you something. She's very concerned about you."

"What are you talking about?"

"When I saw Zara in Martinique—"

"You were in Martinique?"

"Yes. I went to see you, but found her instead," he said with a grin.

"Don't tell me you fell for her."

Mark laughed. "No, she seemed to have found a friend and was well occupied with him. It wasn't that," he told her. "The best way to describe it is that after seeing Zara I realized you were right about us. It would have been nice if it had worked out differently, but we have to accept things as they are. What I feel best about is that I can look at you now and see a friend. Maybe even appreciate you more for the person you really are."

It was a nice sentiment, whether he meant it or not. she thought. Maybe they could be friends, but it wouldn't be easy. Not after what they'd shared. At least the pressure did seem to be off. That was good.

"But we do have important business to discuss," he said. "I'm here at least in part because Zara asked me to bring you a manuscript."

"A *manuscript?*"

"Yes. It's in my bag. Some kind of Mafia exposé that a gangster gave her at JFK. Apparently, the guy mistook her for you."

"Oh, good Lord," she said, putting her hands to her mouth.

"You know about it?"

"The last couple of weeks, some guy was pestering me to look at his hit piece on the New York underworld. The last time I talked to him was just before I was supposed to go to Martinique, but I didn't want to deal with his manuscript then, so I put him off. Apparently, he got impatient and decided to force it on me."

"Well, he ended up giving it to Zara."

"The poor thing," Arianna said. "She got my trip and my problems both."

"The problem is bigger than you might imagine. Zara thinks you're in danger. She was followed to the Caribbean. When I showed up, she was very eager to get the manuscript off her hands."

"But doesn't the Mafia think she still has it? And if so, isn't *she* the one who's in danger?"

Mark took another sip of coffee. "Her friend Alec seemed to be doubling as a guardian angel. He's a former New York cop and, from what I saw, he looked more than willing to take care of her. Still, sooner or later, the bad guys are bound to figure out she doesn't have the manuscript and Zara's convinced they'll come looking for you. I agree with her, and think you've got to take precautions accordingly. In fact, Zara and I both would just as soon you get rid of the thing."

"First I'd like to see it, if you've got it with you."

"I knew you wouldn't be able to resist reading it."

"This *is* my work, Mark."

"Yeah, I know," he said. "I'll go get my bag."

He left the kitchen and Arianna sat stunned. This was so incredible. Suddenly, she recalled that news story she'd seen in the *Times* about the gangster getting killed at the airport. She again wondered if there could be a connection.

Jumping up, she ran to the living room, nearly colliding with Mark in the doorway.

"Whoa," he said, stepping aside.

"I'm going to check something," she said. "I'll be right back."

Arianna found the paper on the table where she'd dropped it earlier and carried it to the kitchen. Mark had taken the manuscript out of his bag and put it on the table, too, but she was preoccupied with the news story and sat down to read it more carefully.

"Sal Corsi," she mumbled. "I wonder if that could be Mr. X."

"Sal Corsi?" Mark said.

"Yes, that's the name of the mobster who was killed at JFK the day Zara was there."

Mark tapped the title page of the manuscript. The byline read "Salvatori Corsi."

"Dear God," she said, looking up at Mark. He seemed none too pleased. She began feeling all shaky inside.

"I think you'd better pack," he said. "It's only a matter of time before they come for you. Especially if they catch up with Zara."

She looked into his eyes, feeling genuine fear for the first time. Then she experienced a very unfamiliar feeling. She wanted the protection of Mark's embrace—his comfort, his strength. Growing up as orphans, she and Zara had been forced to learn to be strong and self-reliant. Far too early in their young lives they'd lost the mother and father they had looked to for protection. This situation amply showed how that loss affected her to this day "All right," she said. "But where should I go?"

"I've been thinking about that ever since I saw Zara. Some friends of my parents, the Bergstroms, have a chalet not too far from here, near Vail. It'll be empty and I know where the keys are. I can take you there until we figure out a solution. If Corsi's dead, maybe all you have to do is put this thing in the hands of the police. Then you'd be out of it since there'd be no reason for the Mob to come after you."

Arianna looked down at the three-inch-thick manuscript, feeling torn. Her fear and her ambition came into conflict. Yes, there was danger, but there was also a tremendous professional opportunity here. "I'm sure you're right about that," she said, "but look what I'd be giving up. Do you have any idea what this means to my career?"

"Arianna, that's nothing compared to your life."

"Who knows how big the exposé is? I certainly won't until I read the book. That's the first thing I've got to do."

"I was afraid you'd say that. But I can't just dump the manuscript on you then ride into the sunset, because I promised Zara that I'd make sure you're safe." He paused for a moment or two, apparently considering options. "How about if I drive you to Vail? You can read the manuscript there. That way I'll keep my promise to Zara. On the way, we can talk. I felt we didn't say goodbye properly and I'd feel better walking away from something like this as friends."

Arianna carefully considered his words. They were measured, reasonable, she didn't hear desperation in them. To the contrary, Mark sounded like a man who cared but was prepared to go on with his life, whether she was on board or not. Why did this feel so different? she wondered. Painful almost. Had she changed? Or had he?

3

MARK WENT to the front window and glanced out at the street. It was quiet, tranquil. A boy on a bicycle rode past, kicking up a flutter of autumn leaves in his wake. A woman stepped out the front door of the house across the street to check her mailbox, then went back inside. He could hear a dog barking in the distance.

How could there be danger in such a peaceful place? he wondered. Yet there was. When he'd heard about Corsi being killed, his concern for Arianna increased tenfold. He wished now he'd never promised to hand over the damn manuscript. But at least she'd agreed to let him take her to Vail. That was a start.

Arianna, who'd been packing, passed him on her way to the laundry room. She cast him a distracted smile but didn't speak. A moment later she walked by again, this time with an armload of clothing.

"I know you're cautious by nature, Mark, but be honest, could we be blowing this out of proportion? I mean, I'm a book editor. How badly could someone want to harm me?"

"I don't think you're the issue, Arianna. It's that manuscript. After talking to Zara, I was concerned. After reading about Corsi, I'm...well, let's just say much more concerned."

Her face twisted into a pensive, questioning expression.

"Listen," he said, "if you think I've got some ulterior motive for exaggerating the danger, you're dead wrong. If you want to know the honest truth, I'd feel a hell of a lot better if the manuscript didn't exist."

"If it didn't exist, you wouldn't be taking me to Vail."

"No, I'd probably be taking you to dinner instead."

Her eyebrows rose in surprise. "You're pretty sure of yourself, Mr. Lindsay."

"Hey, sweetpea, at this point I've got nothing to lose." He grinned at her. "But this is no time to debate my motivations. Get a move on. A Mafia car could pull up at any moment."

"Hmmph," she said, tossing her head as she left the room. "I can't imagine them being any pushier than you!"

Mark was amused. Things felt different and he wasn't entirely sure why. Maybe because he'd stopped telling himself this was not Meredith he was dealing with, it was Arianna. That was so obvious, and yet he'd stumbled through their relationship without paying attention to what he was doing.

He could see now that being himself was much kinder. And the nice thing was, it felt good to zap her when the urge moved him. It still wasn't in him to be hurtful or mean or callous, but neither was he going to worry about her every bruise.

The telephone rang, breaking his train of thought. He heard her answer it in the bedroom, though he couldn't hear what she said. After a couple of minutes she came out.

"That was Zara's friend, Lina Prescott. She tried reaching Zara in Martinique and the manager at the Hotel des Caraïbes told Lina she'd checked out." Arianna looked worried. "Oh, Mark, do you think Zara's all right?"

"I suspect she and her friend are lying low. Remember, I told you he was an ex-cop so I'm sure he's on top of things. In any case, there's nothing we can do from here, so there's no point worrying. But we can take steps to ensure your safety, which is why I'd like to get going."

Arianna nodded. "You're right. But I'm concerned about Lina, too. She seems desperate to talk to Zara, and if I'm not here to relay the message..."

"Eventually, Zara's going to return to your place in New York. I suggest you leave word for her there."

"Good idea. I think I'll write her a note and send it to my apartment. That ought to do the trick."

"Fine. But let's mail it from Vail," Mark said. "I don't want to stick around here a minute longer than necessary."

"Well, all right, I'm almost packed." She started out the door, then stopped. "Mark, can I ask you something?"

"What?"

"*Were* you attracted to Zara?"

He couldn't help the smile that crept across his face.

"*Mark!*"

"Well, she does look an awful lot like you." He gave

her his most innocent smile. "But don't worry, I'd never have done anything to embarrass you."

She gave him a long, appraising look. "A month ago I'd have believed that."

"A month, Arianna, can be a very long time."

MARK WAS on a call to his New York office when she returned to the front room. She checked all the windows and the back door to make certain her sister's house was locked. The suitcases were waiting beside the front door. All that remained was to set the burglar alarm. She listened as Mark gave his final instructions to his administrative assistant. The way he was rushing through his list of things to do told her exactly how eager he was for them to be out of there.

Arianna watched him, enjoying the opportunity to do so unobserved. Not that she hadn't had many such chances while they were engaged, but this Mark, this man who had come to Aspen, didn't seem like her fiancé. Or even the way she'd have expected him to act as an ex-fiancé. *This* Mark intrigued her.

He had the same patrician good looks, chiseled features and narrow nose, but there was something about the set of his jaw that was different. Squarer, more determined. And the soft brown eyes she loved so seemed...harder. There were flashes of mischief—and determination—that she was certain had not been there before.

All in all, she had to say, Mark was edgier. Sexier, if she were dead honest. Or maybe it was simply that danger, even alleged danger, heightened her emotions. That could account for it, too.

"There, that's taken care of," he said, hanging up the phone and turning to her. "I've bought myself a few more days."

"I feel terrible taking you from your work. There's no reason I can't get to Vail on my own."

"And deny me the pleasure?" he said, going to her suitcases.

She picked up the Corsi manuscript. "Pleasure?"

"Maybe I should have said *possible* pleasure. It'll depend on how cooperative you are." He took her cases and she opened the door for him.

"Mark, you aren't suggesting anything...untoward, are you?"

"Not unless you consider formulating a plan of operations untoward."

"A plan of operations? What do you think this is, a war?"

"I hope not. But you never know," he said as he walked out the door.

Arianna locked the door and followed him to his rental car. She watched as he put the cases in the trunk and closed the lid.

"For the first time since I met you, I won't have to worry about stepping on your toes. You see, in breaking our engagement, you've set me free to call them as I see them."

With that he went to the driver's side and opened the door. "Come on," he said. "Hop in."

Arianna was taken aback. In the past he'd always held the passenger door for her, then he'd gone around. In fact, he'd always been so well mannered.

Maybe he really did mean it when he said he didn't have to worry about stepping on her toes.

As soon as she got in and closed the door, he started the engine and they took off. Corsi's book was on her lap. Mark checked the rearview mirror.

"I've been watching the street," he said. "I haven't noticed any suspicious characters. For the moment, anyway, I think you're safe."

She chuckled. "Honestly, Mark. Would you know a suspicious character if you saw one?"

"I watched *The Godfather*, same as everybody else."

"Well, just so I don't wake up with a horse's head next to me," she said wryly.

"You don't own a racehorse, Arianna. I believe that's a prerequisite."

She contemplated him, her intrigue growing. "I think you're actually enjoying this."

"Diversionary tactics, the purpose of which is to keep you off balance."

"You're so confident you're willing to tell me your strategy?"

Mark nodded. "Yeah," he said. Then he smiled.

Arianna was amused. But it also occurred to her that he was getting his way. He was being glib, wry, playful, but he *was* getting his way. And what made it all so amazing was that this was the man she'd broken up with! Yet here he was, determined to protect her from the Big Bad Wolf.

Arianna wondered just how imminent the danger was. Mark hadn't made up that story about Sal Corsi getting killed. But still knowing that did not tell her what he *really* wanted. Her? Maybe. Perhaps even probably. He wasn't going about it as the Mark of old, though. That, as much as anything, had her thoroughly intrigued.

THEY'D BEEN DRIVING for half an hour or so, and had passed Carbondale, which was to the left of the highway. Judging by how fast she was reading, the book was a real page-turner. Mark could feel the energy radiating from her.

"My God," she said, sounding as though she were coming up for air.

"Good or bad?"

"You're not going to like hearing this," she said, "but the exposé is incredible. Sheer dynamite. I can see why the Mob is anxious to put a lid on it. Corsi had the goods on everybody in New York. And I'm going to be right in the middle of it!"

Mark was silent. His worst fears had been realized. But then, he wasn't surprised. How could Arianna not love something as sensational as this?

"Don't worry," she said, obviously trying to rein in her excitement. "This isn't your problem. Really."

"I'm happy for you," he said. "I really am. I know what a big opportunity can be like. I might even feel the same in your shoes. But there's a little problem. What good is success if you're not alive to enjoy it?"

"People who let fear rule their lives never accomplish anything, Mark."

"How well I know. But there are reasonable risks and there are unreasonable risks. It's one thing to be brave, another to be stupid."

"No doubt you're right," she said, a bit of an edge to

her voice. "We agree in principle. Where we may not agree is on where to draw the line."

Mark gritted his teeth. He'd known this would happen. Once they were out of Aspen and she started feeling a little more secure, Arianna's confidence had returned. It was a given. Unfortunately, her judgment had flown right out the window with her fear.

"Look," he said, "I don't think you have any idea what—and more important *who*—you're dealing with. This is not child's play."

She whipped her head around, clearly indignant. "I didn't say it was. Besides, what makes you the expert? You're a banker."

He started to say something but held his tongue. He'd probably already said too much. His preference was to dissuade her, if he could. And if he couldn't, then he'd have to go to Plan B. And it was looking more and more as though that was the way things were headed.

For the next forty-five minutes there were sporadic squeals of delight coming from Arianna. Once she paused to share an anecdote from the manuscript. But the conversation didn't last long.

As they'd driven along Interstate 70, a weather front moved in. Thunderheads were building over the mountains. Arianna had been so engrossed in her reading that she seemed not to have heard the distant rumble. But when the sky darkened and a sharp clap of thunder sounded, she looked up and leaned forward for a view of the sky.

"Looks like we may be in for some rain," she said offhandedly.

"It's been building for the last few miles."

She gave him a woeful look. "I haven't been very good company, I know," she said, "but this is going to be a wonderful project, Mark. I know you can't be happy for me, but please don't give me a hard time."

Mark shook his head, chuckling. "So, you think Mr. Corsi's going to make you rich and famous, huh?"

"Oh, Corsi badly needs an editor, but it's all here, the makings of a blockbuster. And everything's well documented. Look," she said, holding up a slip of paper. "I found this stuck between the pages. Instructions on how to get the original documents from a mail drop in Brooklyn. It'll be what we need to prove the claim of official corruption."

"I don't suppose I have to tell you who'd like to put their hands on it even more than you."

"I think we've both made our feelings clear about that," she said.

"Yeah, right. So what do you propose to do next?"

"I'll need to call Jerry when we get to Vail," she said. "I already know what he'll say, though. He'll tell me to get my butt back to New York pronto."

Mark didn't comment. He'd never cared much for the editor-in-chief at Pierpont Books. Not that Jerry Salter was a bad guy or anything, but he drove Arianna mercilessly, sometimes ruthlessly—not that she was an unwilling victim. An ambitious workaholic employee and a hard-driving boss made for a deadly combination. Mark had tried to tell her it was only a matter of time before things would explode, but Arianna was convinced she'd not only outlast Jerry, but would have his job eventually.

There was more thunder and it started to rain. Mark switched on the windshield wipers. Arianna looked up at the sky.

"Do we have much farther to go?" she asked.

"Only a few miles. I'll have to stop for directions. My parents have been to this place, but I haven't been there in a few years."

"Does it have a telephone?"

"I assume so."

"Maybe I should contact Jerry from a pay phone, just in case. I'll do it when you stop."

Mark frowned. " It might be a good idea if you didn't mention that you're in Vail."

"Why? You aren't suggesting that Jerry would betray me, are you?"

"Intentionally, no. But why give him an unnecessary burden? Besides, if there are corrupt cops and judges involved in this, wiretaps are also a possibility."

"You sound like you know an awful lot about these things. Do you know something you're not telling me, Mark?"

"No comment."

"You're playing games with me again," she said. "Trying to keep me off balance."

"Yeah, but it's getting harder," he said, the corners of his mouth bending.

"At least you're man enough to admit it."

Mark sighed to himself. Yes, Plan B was looking more and more inevitable all the time.

There was a sudden downpour and he had to slow the car. They were on the outskirts of Vail and, through the deluge, he saw an exit ahead with services.

"I'll get off here," he said. "You can make your call and I'll get directions to the chalet."

Arianna reached in back for her jacket. Mark drove down the off-ramp behind a motor home and pulled into a service station. The gas tank was half-full, but he decided to fill up anyway. Arianna put the manuscript on the floor. She'd been silent for a while. Mark hoped his admonitions had sobered her, but he wasn't counting on it.

As he turned off the engine, she glanced over at him. "Don't worry, I won't tell Jerry where I am."

"Thank you."

Arianna looked as though she wanted to touch him, maybe even kiss him. She hesitated, her eyes going back and forth between his. "I want you to know that I'm sorry that this has become a bone of contention."

Mark shrugged. "I'd rather have brought you Richard Gere. But I guess you just have to make do with the Mob."

She got out of the car and went to make her call.

Mark watched her dash to the building through the rain, her sweet little body and slender figure so dear to him. He knew he had her wondering, and that was fine. But he really was in a bind. There was no doubt about the outcome of her call to Jerry. He'd want her to head straight to New York—and into the welcoming arms of the Mafia. So at what point did he resort to strong-arm tactics and risk alienating her forever? Probably sooner rather than later. He'd bet his trust fund on it. But if he was sure of one thing, it was that he wasn't going to bet her life on it, as well.

He finished filling the gas tank and was wiping his hands by the time Arianna returned. She looked glum.

"You okay?"

"Yeah, I'm fine," she replied as she got in the car.

Mark was surprised that she was so downbeat. Maybe he'd been wrong. Maybe Jerry wasn't thrilled with the project, after all. Mark went to pay for the gas, figuring they would talk about it later.

He went into the station to get directions to the Bergstroms' chalet. The route was complicated and he had to take time to study a map. The chalet was in a fairly remote location on a mountainside above Vail, between Eagle's Nest and Game Creek Bowl.

When he returned to the car, Arianna still seemed disheartened. Her strawberry-blond hair and lashes were damp from the rain. She had her jacket on. She didn't look at him, and by the way her shoulders slumped he knew something was troubling her.

"So, what happened?" he said.

"Jerry was thrilled to hear I have Corsi's book. He wanted me to get back to New York pronto, like I thought."

"And? There's obviously more."

Arianna sighed. "It appears you were right about the length the Mafia would go to get this manuscript and Corsi's documents."

"Oh? What happened?"

"Jerry told me our offices were broken into. Mine was completely trashed. They couldn't understand why...until I told Jerry about Corsi's book."

"Forgive me if I say 'I told you so.'"

"Yes, I'm convinced now it's a serious matter and that I'm in danger."

"I never thought I'd actually be happy to hear someone say a thing like that," he said.

"But that doesn't mean I'm giving up on the project. This is just a temporary setback," she said. "I'm a hundred percent committed to doing this."

He groaned. It was painfully clear that logic was useless. Even common sense. "Let's stop beating around the bush," he said. "Give it to me straight. What, specifically, do you plan to do?"

She'd been gazing out at the falling rain, and turned from the window. "Well, I told Jerry I need a few days to think about this."

"And he said?"

"He wanted me to courier the manuscript to him immediately. I refused and that annoyed him."

"What a sweetheart." Mark started the engine.

"I can't sit on it for long, though," she said. "I'm going to use my time to go through the manuscript carefully, do an evaluation and prepare my proposal for the project."

Mark headed back toward the interstate. From his point of view, a few days didn't change things. Arianna wouldn't be any safer in New York then than she would be now. But for him it could be a break. He needed time to put a plan together, and this little setback might afford him the necessary opportunity.

It was still raining, but not as hard as before. They had to go down another mile or so to the central Vail exit.

As he drove up the on-ramp, Arianna sighed, then

said, "Dammit! How can the career opportunity of a lifetime by ruined by a bunch of stupid mobsters?"

"Life's not fair."

"Thanks, Mark, that's a lot of help."

He accelerated to get onto the freeway ahead of an approaching camper. "What do I know? I'm just a banker."

"Seriously. You wouldn't just walk away from this, would you?"

"You really want to know? I'd take Corsi's manuscript right down to the FBI and tell them how to find the documents in the mail drop."

"Wonderful. What about the book? You'd just flush it down the toilet?"

"The book will still be there. Once the bad guys are arrested and indicted and safely out of the way, you can publish your book."

She shook her head. "You simply don't understand how these things work. Timing is everything. Scandals are like fruit. They're perishable."

"Yeah, and so's human life."

"Let's face it, Mark, we just don't see this the same way."

"I know that," he said with a grin. "And I've got my ring back to prove it."

She frowned. "That's not what I meant. You were always very supportive of my career."

"Hate to say it, sweetpea, but those golden days are behind us. Now you're dealing with one mean and stubborn SOB."

She chuckled. "Is that a threat?"

"No. Actually I've got a proposal for you. You've got

what, two, three days before you jump into the frying pan?"

"Before I go back to New York, yes."

"All right, here's the deal. Once you get on that plane, your life is yours to do with it as you wish. While you're with me, I'm in charge of security. We do things my way."

She gave him a sort of double take, as if she was shocked. She didn't comment, but he knew what she was thinking. *What the hell happened to the Mark Lindsay she knew?* Well, the answer was, he was gone, right along with his misguided desire to please and pamper her. The next few days were going his way, whatever it took.

"Fair?" he said.

She slowly nodded. "All right, I guess I can live with that. You can call the shots, but only until I get on that plane."

He repressed a smile. The poor innocent thing. She didn't know it yet, but the plane he put her on wouldn't be headed for New York.

4

ARIANNA HELD the grocery sack, watching the rain as she waited under the overhang at the entrance to the market. Mark had made a dash for the car on the theory that there was no need for both of them to get wet, but the way it was coming down, she knew she'd be soaked if she had to run more than a yard or two.

When he pulled up, she quickly jumped inside, then put the sack in the back seat. Mark's hair and face were wet, as well as his shirt, but he didn't seem uncomfortable in the least.

"Dare I say you've got that housewife look about you, Arianna?"

"Do and I'll smack you," she replied.

Mark laughed. "Admit it. That's the real reason you didn't want to marry me. You couldn't stand the thought of grocery shopping, cooking, cleaning and otherwise taking care of hubby."

"Yeah, sure."

"Don't forget, you did agree we'd be doing things my way the next few days," he said as they drove out of the parking lot.

"Regarding security."

"No, no. You didn't read the fine print. *Everything* I say goes. You may even get to find out what it would be like if you'd married me."

Arianna whacked his arm with the back of her hand. "Shut up, before I start believing you and get nervous."

He laughed.

The lighthearted moment came as a relief. The day had been full of surprises, some of them heavy, though none of them had set her back on her heels as much as Mark himself. Here they were, less than a week after their wedding day, groceries in hand, on their way to a cozy little mountain chalet. The air was rife with sexual tension and only one thing wrong with the picture—a month ago she'd told him goodbye forever.

Or so she thought.

Mark had not been acting like a spurned fiancé. Maybe that was why she felt so dangerously at ease with him. Naturally, she had no intention of throwing herself into his arms. Except for a little flirting at the beginning, this had not been a man-woman thing. And yet, despite the Mafia threat hanging over their heads, this was starting to feel a little too cozy. Warning bells were beginning to go off in her head.

Arianna studied him as he leaned forward to concentrate on the road. She tried to be objective. Mark was the same good-looking man she'd intended to marry. And yes, she was still attracted to him. But the parallels between now and six weeks ago ended there. Given their repartee, and the way the energy was flowing back and forth between them, he might as well have been an attractive stranger. That made her wonder whether she'd missed all this before, or if he'd actually changed that much.

But something else was bugging her, too. He hadn't

told her why he'd gone to the Caribbean. She decided to throw caution to the wind and ask. "Mark, you never told me why you went to Martinique."

He gave her a quick glance, looking bemused by the question.

"I'd really like to know," she said.

"It was a quick decision," he said. "I intended to ask if you really thought you knew what you were doing. But I've figured out the answer."

"Which is?"

"You did the right thing, Arianna. The guy you were engaged to was not the man for you."

What was this? she wondered. False bravado or true insight? "How do you feel about that?"

He negotiated a turn, but managed, despite the distraction, to look contemplative. "I'd say you did us both a favor. As things were, the marriage wouldn't have worked."

As things were, she thought. "Then you must feel uncomfortable being stuck with me now."

"No, actually it's fine."

"Oh, that's right, you said the pressure's off and you're free to be a bastard if you want."

Mark shook his head, laughing. "I don't recall putting it quite that way."

Arianna was starting to feel frustrated. Mark was not exactly being evasive, but she was having trouble getting satisfaction from him. He was like a boxer bobbing and weaving. Why was he doing it? And what did he hope to gain?

Whatever his reasons, it was pointless to agonize over it. All she had to do was relax and put their past from her mind. The solution was probably to think of him as a friend, keep the conversation casual.

"Just out of curiosity," she said, breaking both the silence and her decision to keep things light, "would you say that during our engagement you'd deluded yourself about me?"

"You're asking if I really loved you."

"Well, I wouldn't put it quite that way," she said, embarrassed at being so transparent.

He gave her a sideward glance. "Does it matter?"

"I'm only trying to make conversation," she said. "But to answer your question, no, it doesn't matter. Let's change the subject."

"Fine."

Arianna waited, but he didn't say a word. *Nothing.* She drummed her fingers again. Finally, she blurted it out. "You know, Mark, I am surprised how easily you've gotten over me."

"Oh, so you *do* want to talk about it."

"No!" she said, turning scarlet. "Forget I said that. I don't know what's wrong with me."

"You're obviously feeling guilty."

"*Guilty?*"

Mark threw back his head and laughed. Arianna felt constrained to whack him again, which she did.

"I just want you to know I've suffered over this," she said. "I agonized long and hard before I decided to give back your ring."

"Hey, sweetpea, nobody's wrong in situations like this. We're both doing the best we can with what we've got. Now, I suggest you forget about the past and start thinking about what you're going to fix me for dinner."

"Bastard."

He chuckled. "I think you're feeling better already."

Weather conditions worsened and Mark continued to struggle with his driving. The rain would let up at times, but then it would come down in a torrent.

They wound their way up the mountainside and when they came to a split in the road, Mark studied the situation before choosing which way to go. After another fifteen minutes, they took a side gravel road and came to a parking area. There weren't any cars, which was no surprise considering the season. He parked near the stairway that led to the path accessing the chalets and pointed out the name Bergstrom on a mailbox.

"This is the place, all right."

They decided there was no point in sitting around waiting for the rain to let up. Mark got their bags. Arianna stuffed Corsi's manuscript into one of them, grabbed the sack of groceries and they made a run for the chalet.

It was not only miserably wet, it was cold. As they hurried, Arianna imagined them warming themselves by a cozy fire, former lovers, stuck together by circumstances. It was almost as if Mark had planned the whole thing. For a brief moment she wondered if that was possible. But, no, the manuscript was real. So was the article about Sal Corsi's murder. Maybe fate simply had a bizarre sense of humor.

Arianna moved as fast as she could, though the bag was unwieldy enough that she couldn't run very fast. Squinting into the blowing rain, she saw a roofline through the trees. The sack was already wet. Visions of it falling apart went through her mind. The chalet was just coming into view when she tripped over a root and landed on her behind. The groceries landed with a splat. The sack disintegrated and the milk was oozing over the muddy ground.

Mark immediately stopped and turned. There was concern on his face until he saw she was all right. Arianna looked up at him as he broke into a smile.

"Make one wisecrack and so help me I'll kill you."

He looked throroughly amused. "How could I make light of such a pathetic sight?"

"Careful."

He put down the cases and came over to help her up. They were very close, their faces only inches apart. Arianna looked into his eyes. He looked at her mouth. It was as though neither of them were aware of the rain.

"Know what?" he finally murmured. "You've got mud all over your face."

Embarrassed, Arianna wiped her cheek with the back of her hand.

"No," he said. "You're only making it worse."

Then he took his handkerchief and wiped away the mud. It was a terribly intimate gesture. She couldn't remember him ever doing anything like that before.

"Is this part of the security service?" she asked.

"There's more in the fine print than you'd imagine." He let go of her and looked down at the scattered groceries. "Let's leave this," he said. "I'll come back for it."

With that, he picked up the suitcases and they headed toward the chalet. When they reached the porch, Arianna stood under the overhang while Mark went to a nearby window to hunt for the key behind the shutter. Muddy and shivering, she watched him.

"At least you can't say our post-engagement isn't exciting," he said, returning to the porch and unlocking the door.

They went inside. Mark took their suitcases and set them down. She tiptoed in, closing the door behind her and looked around. Massive brown leather sofas faced each other in front of a stone fireplace. There were Navajo rugs hung on the walls and Native American pottery and baskets were scattered around the room. Fortunately the floor was wood, so she would not have a horrendous time cleaning up their muddy footprints.

"Get out of those wet clothes and I'll find you a towel," Mark said.

Without waiting for a reply, he headed off to find the bathroom. Arianna was not eager to strip, but she was even less eager to stay in her wet clothes. She took off everything except her bra and panties. They were wet, too, but she wasn't about to remove them. At least not yet. She was hugging herself as Mark returned with a big fluffy bath towel.

"Oh, this is heaven," she said as he wrapped it around her.

He vigorously rubbed her back, then took a corner of the towel and dabbed her face. Arianna remembered a similar gesture when they'd taken a shower at his place. They'd ended up making love, not even bothering to dry their hair.

Clutching the towel under her chin, she looked up at him through her wet lashes. Her teeth were chattering, but she had a tremendous desire for him to take her into his arms and hold her. He reached up and, taking her chin between his fingers, said, "I'll try to find something in the kitchen to put the groceries in." Then he headed off.

Arianna felt a wave of disappointment. A loss. She wanted Mark to be more interested in her than the damn groceries. But then, maybe he knew exactly what he was doing. The point of all this might be to torture her. If so, he was doing a fine job of it.

ARIANNA STOOD under the spray of water, feeling like a new woman. She had been certain that after Mark returned with the groceries, he would try to keep her off balance by acting romantic again. But it hadn't worked that way. Instead, he'd surprised her with his business-like attitude. He'd turned on the water heater. Then, knowing it would be a while before the tank got hot, they made dinner and ate by the fire, which Mark had built while the food was cooking.

She had changed into her sweats and Mark had put on dry clothes, but she'd craved a hot shower to get the chill from her bones. So while Mark had cleared the dishes, she'd gone to the bathroom to shower.

As she soaped herself, Arianna thought about the meal they'd shared. It had been strange. This was, after all, the man she'd once planned to spend the rest of her life with. Yet, he wasn't the same man at all. It confounded her that she couldn't get a handle on him. Nor were her feelings about him clear. One minute she wanted it to be the best it had ever been between them. The next she would take a reality check and remind herself where they were, and why.

When the water got tepid, Arianna knew it was time to get out. After she'd toweled off, she put on her terry robe and partially dried her hair, deciding to let it finish drying by the fire. The wisest thing would be to put her sweats back on, but she returned to the front room in her robe. Mark was sprawled on the large rug in front of the stone fireplace.

"Well," he said, looking surprised to see her in her robe and bare feet. "Is she a new woman?"

"Very new and feeling much better, thanks," she said, dropping onto the rug next to him, but not too close. "I thought I'd finish drying my hair by the fire."

She fluffed her damp curls. As she did, the lower part of her robe opened slightly, exposing her thigh. She modestly covered herself, but Mark had noticed.

"What do you have on under that?" he asked unabashedly.

"Nothing," she replied without hesitation.

Mark's silence made her wonder what he was thinking. She became uncomfortable. "If it bothers you, I can always put on my sweats."

"Do I look like a fool?" he said with a wink. Then he fell silent again.

Arianna hugged her knees and stared at the fire. Although the unspoken messages were strong, she couldn't read them clearly. Mark's demeanor was calm, but she sensed that under the surface there was a lot going on. Was it anger, resentment, regret, desire, love? She couldn't be sure. Nor could she leave the question unasked.

"Mark, would you please tell me why you've changed?"

He rolled onto his side, facing her, his head resting on his hand.

"I suppose I owe you that," he said. "It's nothing mysterious. When I saw Zara in Martinique, she said something that opened my eyes."

"What was it?"

He paused, as if considering his words carefully. "Let me put it this way," he said finally. "She helped me see that I wasn't being myself. I was playing a role and it ended up being counterproductive."

"How so?"

He chuckled and put his hand on her bare foot, caressing it as though it were a kitten. She repressed a shiver, liking his touch.

"After talking to Zara, I realized I'd been treating you as if you were Meredith. I burdened our relationship with some old baggage. I suppose people do that all the time. In this case, it proved to be costly. But you live and learn."

"Meredith, the girl you were engaged to right after college? The one who died?"

"Yes. I was preoccupied with trying to avoid the same mistakes I'd made with her. In the process, I wasn't being true to myself."

"What mistakes?"

He gave her a skeptical look. "You really want to talk about this?"

"Yes, I want to understand."

"It's very simple," he said. "I blamed myself for what went wrong...for her death...and resolved never to make the same mistake again. I ended up overcompensating and you...we...suffered because of it."

"She died in an automobile accident, didn't she?"

"Yes, but what you didn't know was that I held myself responsible. Meredith was driving and she was alone and upset. Earlier in the evening I'd hurt her. We'd gone to a party, argued and she left in tears. I didn't do anything to stop her. I let her go and I never saw her alive again."

"That's tragic, I grant you, but it's not your fault. People have arguments. That doesn't make you responsible for her death."

"In retrospect I see that. I suppose I even knew it at the time. But I also knew if I'd been more sensitive to her needs, more caring and less selfish, she wouldn't have died. I was young and full of myself and I hurt her. And after she died I vowed that I would put the happiness and well-being of the people I loved first."

"And you overdid it."

"Exactly."

For the first time, Arianna understood. Mark had tried too hard to please her because of the emotional scars he carried. "I wish you'd said something, Mark."

"The irony is, I didn't know that's what was happening. I sensed you pulling away, but instead of backing off, I tried even harder to give you the attention I thought you needed."

Arianna stared into the fire. "And I didn't tell you what I was feeling."

"I was the one who'd misplayed my hand."

"No, people have a responsibility to communicate their feelings. In a way, I let *you* down."

"I should have been true to myself. It's fine to be considerate, but you've also got to be honest. The worst thing you can do is to try to be somebody you aren't."

She shook her head. "And we owe this great insight to my sister."

"It should have been obvious," he said. "But I guess it wasn't—until it was too late." Then he got up and put a couple more logs on the fire.

Arianna watched as a column of sparks rose up the chimney. Here they were, calmly having a conversation they should have had months ago. She knew she had as much responsibility for that failing as he. But she hadn't realized what the problem was any more than he had. The question now was, if Mark had been putting on an act all those months, who was he really? This guy who'd brought her the manuscript and who was trying to save her from the Mafia?

"It's not too late to be compassionate toward one another," she said.

"True," he said, leaning over, taking her foot, and kissing the top of her toes. A violent shiver went through her, but the sensation pleased her.

"Is this your idea of compassion, Mr. Lindsay?" she asked, amused.

"Let's just say I haven't been able to get it out of my mind that you don't have anything on under that robe."

She curled her legs under her and smoothed the hem of the robe. "I never should have told you. Or better still, I should have gotten dressed."

"There's a reason for it, Arianna."

"Are you saying I'm trying to tempt you?"

"Are you?"

"Of course not! I just wanted to let my hair dry by the fire," she said, fluffing her curls again. "I know you're a gentleman. God, I've virtually put my life in your hands, haven't I?"

"But which me? The guy putting on the act all those months, or the real me?"

She laughed nervously.

"It's a serious question," he said.

"Come on, Mark, you may have repressed certain things and forced others, but you aren't Dr. Jekyll and Mr. Hyde."

"You're sure?"

She smiled, looking down at him. But he wasn't smiling back. "Mark...come on. I have noticed a difference, but..."

"What if you discovered that I'm the polar opposite of what you thought? Say I peel off the mask I've been wearing and you find a completely different man there?"

She smoothed the lapel of her robe, closing it at the neck. "Now you're teasing me."

"I'm having a little fun with it, I admit. But you know the old saying, 'Where there's smoke, there's fire.'"

He took her hand. As Arianna watched, he pulled her fingers to his mouth and kissed them. This, she decided, was a seduction. And a woman did not allow herself to be seduced by a man after breaking their engagement. Yet she wasn't at all sure she wanted him to stop.

"There's one thing I absolutely, positively did not fake," he said. "My attraction to you was a hundred percent genuine. I always made love with you for the pleasure."

She watched as he toyed with her fingers. "Does that mean the Mr. Hyde character who brought me to this hideaway is faking it now?"

Mark firmly grasped her wrist and gave her arm a tug, pulling her over on top of him. "That remains to be seen."

She looked down into his smiling eyes as he wrapped his arms around her waist, trapping her. "Dr. Jekyll might have been a little too nice," she said, "but at least I trusted him."

"But I thought you liked living dangerously, Ari. I thought that poor bastard you were engaged to was too staid, too conventional, too suffocating."

"Whereas you wouldn't hesitate to take advantage of me?"

"It's easy enough to find out," he said. "Are you just dying for me to seduce you?"

"No!"

He shrugged. "Well, I could care less. Jekyll might have, but I don't."

She smiled. "Mark, you're really outdoing yourself. If it wasn't so funny, I'd be impressed."

"Dangerous words," he said. He gazed into her eyes as the firelight played on his face. "I take that as a challenge."

Then he kissed her. It was a tender, seductive kiss at first, but then it grew more passionate. Mark reached between them, loosening the tie of her robe so he could cup her breast. His tongue probed her mouth.

Digging her fingers into his hair, she pulled his face

back to see his eyes. "Didn't it occur to you this might not be a good idea?" she breathed.

"The thought went through my mind," he replied hoarsely, giving her lower lip a kiss. "But I didn't dwell on it for long."

With that, he kissed each corner of her mouth. Then, before she could say a word, he kissed each breast. Arianna moaned, closing her eyes as his lips trailed across her abdomen and traveled languorously from one hipbone to the other. His raspy tongue nearly drove her to the edge. Her excitement rose higher and higher and she thought of nothing but the pleasure until he paused, took her hand and kissed it.

She lay there, her breathing uneven, wondering how this could have happened. They should have been past this by now, but she'd fallen into it as though they'd never parted. She couldn't say this wasn't the lover she'd known, but he *did* seem different. She sensed more abandon, more fire. Or was it her?

When Mark glanced up at her, she caressed his cheek. "You haven't lost your touch," she said.

"Nor have you."

"But aren't we just creating unnecessary complications?"

"I haven't put any conditions on this," he said, running the tip of his index finger around her navel. "Have you?"

"No, Mark, but making love out of weakness is not good."

He pressed his lips to the taut skin between her navel and her downy fringe. "You can hardly feel guilty if you can't help yourself," he murmured.

She could feel his hot breath as his face moved lower. A charge went through her. "Damn you, Mark," she whispered raggedly. "This isn't fair."

Once more, he drew his mouth across her hip and down the outside of her thigh. "Being fair is not my intent."

He slowly parted her thighs and drew his tongue up the soft inner flesh of first one leg, then the other. She stared back through heavily lidded eyes, letting herself revel in each kiss, each stroke of his tongue. Time seemed endless, as though each second would last an eternity...or more, if that was what they wanted.

In a very small part of the back of her mind, Arianna realized that he was having the wedding night she'd denied him— and herself. But somehow, ulterior motives did not matter just then. Nothing did, except the exquisite sensation.

Mark pulled away from her long enough to undress. She watched the firelight flicker over his chest. When he was naked, he drew his hand between her legs until his finger found her center. The connection sent another electric charge through her. Her breathing grew shallow and started coming in gasps.

She knew he had to be gloating. She hadn't offered any resistance. But the time for protest was long past. Taking his wrist, she pressed his hand against her, arching to meet his touch.

Arianna closed her eyes, wanting him. But which him? The man who was making love with her was familiar *and* unfamiliar. Oh, he had the same features, but this wasn't the man she knew any more than Zara was her. *This* Mark was a man who would always get exactly what he wanted.

As Mark eased himself over her, she opened her legs for him to enter her. And as she felt him slide into her, she knew he'd won.

But then, so had she.

And when she came, Arianna cried out. Spent, Mark collapsed onto her. She listened to the sounds of rain on the roof and the crackle of the fire. She felt the warmth of his skin on hers. Most of all, Arianna noticed the beat of his heart, thudding in unison with hers.

For a while, she didn't want to think about what had happened, only how she felt. But the quieter her body became, the more her mind intruded. Why had she given this up? Then, as moments stretched into minutes, she realized that this wasn't what she'd given up, because this wasn't Mark Lindsay—at least, not the one she'd known.

The old Mark would have been professing his love at this point. The new Mark hadn't so much as mentioned the word. But that was okay. Love wasn't what this was about. This was about something as yet undefined, involving a man she didn't fully know.

5

MARK SAT ON THE STOOP, listening to the birds and the soft wind in the pines. He felt great. He had never had an unsatisfying sexual experience with Arianna, but last night had been exceptional. He couldn't recall her throwing herself into lovemaking with such abandon, once she'd put her initial misgivings behind her. They'd made love a second time, in his bed, and she'd seemed even hungrier for him than before. Afterward, though, she'd gotten very quiet, finally stealing away to her room as he dozed off.

She was still asleep when he'd awakened, which meant he'd have to wait a while before he found out what she was thinking. He expected repercussions. After all, she'd dismissed him from her life only to fall into his bed a month later. Things like that took a little explaining, even to oneself.

But for the moment, he was content to let it be her problem. Mark sighed, aware for the first time how liberating that was. Before his conversation with Zara, he'd have assumed responsibility for Arianna's happiness. Now he was letting her fend for herself. Of course, that was for her benefit as much as his. Good relationships were based on mutuality. That had been a painful lesson, but it was already paying dividends.

Mark listened, wondering if he might have heard her

stirring, but when he didn't hear anything else, he concluded that she was in no hurry to put in an appearance. Even the aroma of fresh coffee hadn't lured her down. So he'd come outside.

The brisk air said that autumn had arrived. He liked this time of year. He liked having some time away from his life. And he liked being with Arianna. The only thing he didn't like was that it was temporary. One night of lovemaking was nothing to turn up your nose at, but what did it really mean?

The key, he told himself, was being willing to accept the fact that once they were back home, they might never see each other again. And even more important, Arianna had to sense that he accepted that. What a paradox! It was like that old saying that you couldn't really possess a thing until you set it free.

"Mark?" It was Arianna calling from inside.

He got up and went into the chalet. Arianna was in the front room, dressed in jeans and a sweater, looking more beautiful than ever.

"Good morning," he said, trying to sound chipper. "Sleep well?"

"Yes, I did." She seemed a touch embarrassed.

"How about you?" she asked.

"Yes, fine."

"That's good."

Mark could see this was on a par with a first "morning after" with a new lover. He liked that. It meant a fresh start. "Coffee's made," he told her.

"I thought I smelled it."

As they went into the kitchen, Mark admired the

way the jeans molded her figure. "How about some scrambled eggs?" he said.

"If you're making some, I'll have a bite, but don't make them just for me." She took a mug from the counter and poured herself coffee. "Want any, Mark?"

"I'm fine for now."

Arianna perched herself on one of the stools at the kitchen counter. Mark started cracking the eggs into a bowl. He wasn't much of a cook, but when one of them stayed over, he'd usually make breakfast. Ari was more the dinner type, though they frequently went out. Of course, that was then.

He glanced over at her. She was sipping her coffee, but they made eye contact.

"Could we talk about last night?" she asked.

"We can talk about anything you like, sweetpea. Fire away." Searching in the cupboard, he found chili powder and dried parsley and garlic salt, but no ground thyme—his secret ingredient. He'd have to make do.

Arianna took another sip of coffee before she began. "Well...as an observation...I'd say we haven't lost any of our old spark."

"That's fair enough," he said, setting a skillet on the stove. He finished cracking the eggs, added spices and began whisking.

"Good sex isn't a whole relationship. I'm not denigrating you by saying this, but last night hasn't changed my feelings about us. I mean, I'd look awfully superficial if I were to say, 'Oh, great sex, maybe we should reconsider.' Does that make sense?"

Mark checked the pan, turned down the heat and

added the eggs. "Sure. Everybody knows one rose does not a summer make."

"It isn't a matter of roses or no roses. It never has been. God, if people married because of sexual compatibility, there'd be no contest. What I mean is...I guess...well..." She fell silent, shifted uncomfortably, and then took another sip of coffee.

"I have a feeling you're trying to say something." He smiled. "So why not get right to the point?"

"Okay," she said, resolutely setting down her mug. "I don't think there should be any more fun and games. Last night was great, as I said, but it complicates things." She sighed painfully. "Can't we just act like friends instead of lovers?"

"Sure."

He slid bread into the toaster. When the toast popped up, he put a slice on each plate, divided up the scrambled eggs and set one plate in front of Arianna along with a stick of butter and a knife. Then he handed her a fork and took one for himself.

They ate for a while in silence.

"I'd forgotten how good your eggs were," she said at length. "It must be the mountain air. They say it makes everything seem better."

"Oh, so that's what happened last night." Mark grinned.

She gave him a look.

He shrugged. "What can I say? Temptation's a terrible thing."

"You're enjoying every minute of this," she protested. "And I don't think you've taken a word I said seriously."

He held up his hands in surrender. "Sorry, I'm really going to try. Promise."

She shook her head and glanced toward the window. "Looks like a nice day."

"Yup. Storm's over, sun's out. It's a beautiful day."

"And I've got a career-making book in my hot little hands."

Mark didn't say a word, but he could see now the manuscript was going to be her refuge. No surprise there. Arianna had often used work to protect herself from personal problems. Truth be known, in the past, he'd always been a little jealous of her passion for her career. Now that he was letting go, he told himself the best thing to do was to be happy for her. The trouble was, this particular book posed a danger. How he dealt with that was his single biggest challenge—bigger, in a way, than their relationship itself.

"Want to hear something funny," Arianna said wistfully. "Before Zara went to Martinique, she and Laura and Darcy had dinner at Madame Wu's Destiny House."

"The Chinese restaurant that hands out fortunes that come true?"

"The very one." She paused dramatically and looked up at him. "Zara brought a fortune home for me, because I couldn't go with them that night."

Mark took a bite of eggs. "What was it?"

"Never judge a book by its cover."

He chuckled. "Not too original."

"No," she said, "but apropos, don't you think? After all, I thought Corsi was a phony when he first contacted me. And now it looks as if he's presented me with the opportunity of a lifetime."

"At the cost of his own life," Mark added, breaking off a corner of his toast.

"You aren't going to let me forget that, are you?" she said somberly.

"The danger is the one thing I can't let go of. Even if you told me you were going to marry some other guy tomorrow, I'd still feel responsible for getting you through this." Mark felt his emotion rising, but couldn't help himself.

"Mark, I think this project is what you need to let go of. Not me. I'm sure you're overreacting."

"And I'm sure you're underreacting."

Arianna took a bite of toast. "Are we having a fight?"

"Possibly." Mark got the coffeepot and filled her mug. "I hate to say it, but this exposé may end up being our irreconcilable difference."

"I do have the option of telling you to mind your own business, you know."

"And I have the option of keeping you here."

Her eyebrows rose. "Against my will?"

Mark realized he wasn't going to be able to finesse this. "Please," he said, "make a copy of the manuscript before you turn it over to the FBI so you will have something to work with. Lay low while they conduct their investigation. Then surface when it's safe."

"Mark, you know darn well it could take months before they'd let me publish. Anyway, I have to get to New York to locate those supporting documents Corsi hid."

He took a deep breath before he spoke. "Should I conclude there's no chance of changing your mind?"

"This is my work, Mark. Thank you for caring, but..."

"Butt out?"

"I'm a big girl," she said.

Yes, she was a big girl. And a determined one. But if he couldn't drive a little sense into her thick head, he'd be forced to fall back on his other options. Even if she ended up hating him for it.

IT ONLY TOOK Arianna another couple of hours to finish reading Sal Corsi's book and she was more excited than ever. Smiling, she stretched out on the sofa. She planned to go through the manuscript again, this time more carefully, making notes as she read. Some good ideas on the editorial approach she'd take had already come to mind.

After breakfast, Mark had left the chalet, saying there were some things he wanted to take care of in town. She couldn't imagine what he needed to do there, unless it was use a fax machine, but she didn't bother to ask. She had plenty to worry about with the manuscript. There was also the problem of getting the necessary permissions from Corsi's estate, but she'd leave that to Jerry and the lawyers. It was another reason to get back to New York pronto, though.

She'd never been more excited about a project. Yet there was a grain of sand in her shoe. Memories of the night before simply wouldn't go away.

It wasn't like her to lose control that way. Which was especially odd considering she'd rejected Mark once.

She'd tried to get through the morning without being too humiliated, but there was no doubt in her mind that she'd face more temptation down the road.

Of course, the best way to handle that was to avoid it. But she'd promised to give Mark a few days to sort out the Mafia threat—a promise she was already beginning to regret. Arianna knew she couldn't let herself get sidetracked. Concentrate on the book, she told herself. Concentrate on the book!

By midafternoon Arianna was already a quarter of the way through her second pass at the manuscript. There was still no sign of Mark. As she'd eaten lunch, she'd pondered his absence. What could have detained him? Surely he hadn't encountered the Mob. True, Zara had passed the book off to him, but the chances that the bad guys had been watching them at the time were slim. Weren't they?

She checked her watch again. Mark had been gone for more than six hours and hadn't so much as phoned. That wasn't at all like him. Which made her wonder if something *had* happened. What if the Mafia had grabbed Zara and forced her to admit that she'd given the manuscript to Mark? Knowing he would head for Aspen, it wouldn't have been hard to bribe the rental-car companies to find out what make of automobile he was driving. She and Mark had been seen in Vail getting gas and groceries. Heavens, they had even asked for directions to this place. Even now, the Mafia could have caught up with him!

Arianna shivered at the thought. Then she told herself to get a grip. She'd spent the entire day reading about hits and retaliations and crime wars. She was so inundated with Corsi's saga of corruption and violence that she wasn't thinking straight.

Curled on the sofa, Arianna turned her mind back to her work. She'd fall into what she was doing for a time, only to remember Mark and look at her watch anxiously. Finally, around four o'clock, she heard the front door opening. Mark came in with a small grocery sack in his arms.

"Where have you been?" she asked, showing her concern.

"I picked up a couple of steaks for dinner," he replied.

"It took seven hours?"

He gave her a wry smile. "You noticed?"

"Mark, you're the one who's been insisting we're in a dangerous situation. I was worried something happened to you."

"Fear not, I'd have taken a poison capsule before I'd tell them where you are."

"It's not funny," she insisted, though she laughed anyway. "Seriously, what were you doing?"

"Oh, I had some calls to make, and while I was out I poked around Vail. Anyway, I thought you'd relish the peace and quiet."

"I'd have enjoyed it more if you'd let me know you'd be gone so long."

Mark sat on the arm of the chair across from her. "Now I understand what they mean when they say adjusting to marriage can be difficult. I'm being cross-examined and I'm only a spurned fiancé."

She realized he was right and felt embarrassed. Still,

her first instinct was to defend herself. "I'd have thought you'd be glad I worried about you."

"I'm flattered, but I wish you were half as appreciative of *my* concern for *you*."

"I shouldn't have brought it up."

Smiling, Mark got to his feet. "How much longer are you going to work? I got a nice Bordeaux to go with the steaks, and some hors d'oeuvres and a bottle of Californian Chardonnay for starters."

Her defenses went up. "You aren't planning a special evening, are you, Mark?"

"Just good food and conversation."

She wasn't sure whether to believe him or not. He might be hoping for a replay of the previous night, which would have been a nice idea in one way, but bad in another.

"I think I'll pass," she said. "I'll probably try to work some more this evening."

"Suit yourself, sweetpea," he said, heading to the kitchen.

Sweetpea, she thought, recalling pleasantly how much she'd liked the nickname. The fact he still used it proved he was toying with her—teasing, chiding, being provocative. Well, he wasn't exactly sweeping her into his arms and carrying her off to bed, but he *was* playing with her, honoring the letter of their agreement but not the spirit.

At some point he would make a move on her, she was fairly certain. But she was determined not to slip again. After all, it made absolutely no sense to break off with a man, then proceed to become his lover. Probably the best way to stay on track was to keep all discussion to the situation at hand—like when they should return to New York. Setting aside the manuscript, she went to the kitchen. Mark was putting away the food.

"I know it's a sore subject," she said, "but I need to make plane reservations. When are you planning on going back, and can I hitch a ride to Denver?"

Mark turned to face her, not pleased, judging by his expression, but resigned. "I thought I'd head out day after tomorrow."

Arianna was hoping they might leave in the morning. But she didn't want to press him. He'd been awfully good about helping her and a little flexibility on her part would be a good public-relations gesture, if nothing else. "An evening flight?"

"That would work."

He stuck the Chardonnay in the freezer and finished putting away the groceries, except for the hors d'oeuvres—little finger sandwiches—which he started arranging on a plate. "Wine will be cool in twenty minutes. Sure you wouldn't like to sip while you read?"

It was a tempting offer. She went to the counter and climbed onto one of the stools. "I'm tempted, I admit."

Mark glanced up from his work, smiling. "When happy hour rolls around, even the worst workaholics can succumb."

He seemed to home in on her vulnerabilities. Already, she found herself wanting to rationalize. She'd worked hard; to relax a little wouldn't be the end of the world as long as she was careful. But would she be able—and willing—to keep him in check, especially if she kept sending the wrong signals?

Arianna had to give him credit for neutralizing her defenses so easily. Mark had always been charming, but now he was charming and...something else. Elusive, maybe. It gave him a kind of edge. One she was drawn to. Strongly.

She thought about it and decided the reason she was succumbing was that without his ring on her finger, the pressure was off. Because *she* had let go, he *seemed* different. But why was she thinking about him? She admonished herself to stick to her game plan.

"So, were you able to get a lot done by phone?" she asked.

"The important things."

"I figured you probably needed a fax machine since there's a phone here."

He glanced up at her again. "Not really."

Was he being circumspect, or was it her imagination? "You've devoted an awful lot of time to me," she said. "I hope it hasn't messed things up for you at the office."

"I'm treating this as an unscheduled vacation, Arianna."

"That's good."

He'd finished arranging the finger sandwiches and had dumped some stuffed olives into a bowl. He pushed both over in front of her. "Care to sample the goods?"

She plucked an olive from the bowl and popped it into her mouth. "So, since you got your ring back, have you dated at all?"

She could see by his expression that her question had taken him by surprise. But he quickly recovered.

"No, I'm still in mourning. I figure I won't be over you for another...oh...two weeks, maybe." He shook his head solemnly.

Her eyes narrowed. "Well, I hope you come out of it gleeful."

"I'm doing my best." He munched on an hors d'oeuvre. "How about you, sweetpea? Fall madly in love with Richard Gere?"

"That was work. Exclusively."

Mark scoffed. "The man must be a better actor than I thought."

"Are you complimenting me?"

He reached across the counter and lightly touched her cheek. "Why not?"

Arianna smiled into his eyes, wondering why this was feeling so good. During their engagement it had never been unpleasant. But now Mark had her wanting more, even though she knew darn well she shouldn't be with him. It was probably a case of being lured by the forbidden.

"Let me ask a hypothetical question," Mark said, picking up another sandwich. "Do you think we're better suited as lovers or spouses?"

"What made you think of that?"

He gave her an inquiring look. "Want the truth?"

"Of course."

"I was reading thoughts of that nature on your face a few moments ago."

She took another olive. "Well...if I was in the market for a lover, you'd be an excellent choice. Let me put it that way. *Hypothetically* speaking, that is." She tossed the olive in the air and caught it in her mouth. "But that's not really what you wanted to know. Is it?"

He gave her a quirky, noncommittal smile.

She contemplated him, frustrated that she couldn't pin him down. "There was more to your question than that, Mark, and you know it. Why don't you just admit what this is really about?"

"Which is?"

She ran her fingers absently over the countertop. "This morning I said no more sex and now you're try-ing to seduce me, just to prove you're irresistible. You may be suave, Mark, but you're also transparent."

He shrugged helplessly, though she knew that, too, was an act.

"Oh, it would be easy for me hop in bed with you and it wouldn't ruin my life or anything," she said. "But what about tomorrow morning? Children suc-cumb to the need for instant gratification, not adults."

He nodded thoughtfully. "You make a very convinc-ing argument, Arianna."

"Do I? I'm not so sure you buy it. Deep down, I don't think you care a tinker's damn about how I'd feel to-morrow."

With that, Mark's expression turned hard. "Hey, we were engaged for months and all I did was care. In fact, I cared too damn much. The difference now is that I'm willing to let *you* take care of *yourself*."

She drew a long breath. "How can I possibly object to that? Right?"

"Then maybe we don't have as big a problem as you make it sound," he said evenly.

Mark brushed crumbs from the counter. From his

expression, she could tell he was getting control of himself again. She watched as he went to the freezer, took out the wine and opened the bottle. Then he found two glasses and poured some wine into each, setting them in front of her.

"I'm having some Chardonnay," he said. "If you want any, it's entirely up to you."

As she watched, Mark picked up one glass and took a sip, his eyes on her all the while. She stared back, feeling her resolve crumble. Why bother putting up a fight only to give in later? she asked herself.

She took the glass and brought it to her lips, staring back defiantly. "I've only got one thing to say to you, Mark Lindsay—don't gloat."

The corner of his mouth twitched. "Sweetpea, I wouldn't dream of it."

Arianna took another sip. She didn't need one of Madame Wu's fortune cookies to tell her how the rest of the evening would go. It was a foregone conclusion.

6

WHEN ARIANNA AWOKE the next morning, Mark was not beside her. She was relieved, in a way, because she was embarrassed to think she was facing the same problem as the day before. Two glasses of Chardonnay. Bordeaux with dinner. Another fire. Mark's seductive touch. The result was destined from the moment she'd picked up that first glass of wine. He had known she was his for the asking, making her feel wanton, even decadent, which served to heighten the excitement.

As the night before, they'd made love twice—once with her bent over the arm of the chair in front of the fire, the second time with her astride him in her bed. It had been highly sexual, but there had been a tenderness, especially when Mark held her in his arms afterward all night long.

Though he still hadn't told her he loved her, love was in his fingertips. She'd liked that a lot because she didn't want this to be just a sexual thing, though she wasn't sure how to define her desires. Mainly she hadn't wanted to think about that because it led to a lot of hard questions, like why in the hell she'd broken off with him in the first place.

Now, much as she hated to admit it, she was afraid that Mark might have ulterior motives. What if this whole thing had been concocted to humiliate and get even with her? What if the second she admitted she'd made a mistake, he laughed in her face and walked away? It was hard to imagine such a thing because Mark was not cruel. She didn't expect him to do that, or anything else that was truly unkind, but she'd insisted on breaking up, and therefore bore the burden of responsibility for what had happened.

Mark had given no indication of his feelings. They were both taking a wait-and-see position. Probably the thing to do was assume that their two magical nights had been an aberration and see how things went once they were back home. An evening or two in familiar surroundings and she should be able to figure out who she was dealing with—the Mark Lindsay she'd been engaged to and who had suffocated her with attention, or the one who'd come to Colorado to rescue her.

Arianna got out of bed. She sniffed the air but couldn't detect the inviting scent of fresh-brewed coffee. Maybe Mark hadn't put the pot on yet.

She slipped on her robe and went looking for him, but he wasn't in the second bedroom or the front room or the kitchen. She stepped outside and checked the porch. He wasn't there, either. She called his name. There was no response. Figuring he'd gone for a walk, she decided to shower and get dressed.

Half an hour later when she emerged from her room, there was still no Mark. She looked around the house more carefully, thinking he might have left a note, but there was nothing. Lord, he couldn't have abandoned her, could he? Checking his room, she found his clothes were still there. Maybe he'd gone into town again, but it seemed rather early for such a trip.

Trying not to be too concerned, she made toast. She found a small jar of instant decaf and made some coffee, as well. After she'd finished eating, there was still no sign of Mark, so she started to work on the manuscript. She'd plodded along for a couple of hours, still trying not to worry when, to her relief, Mark came in the door.

"If it's another woman, I don't want to hear about it," she teased.

He grinned, but only momentarily. "Sorry, but I didn't expect to be gone so long. I went into town so that Marcia could fax me a P&L statement, and while I was there...well, I think I might have been followed," he said, sounding concerned.

A stab of fear went through her. "Followed?"

"By some men in town. I tried to be careful when I left so that they wouldn't tail me. I'm not positive, but I think I was successful."

She put aside the manuscript and got to her feet. "Oh, Mark, do you think it's..."

"Them? Possibly."

"What'll we do?"

"I don't know that there's anything to do," he said. "Except be careful."

She shivered and Mark came to her, putting his arms around her. He felt safe and inviting.

"Don't worry, Arianna," he said. "We'll get through this somehow."

The words were reassuring, but if she was in danger

in the middle of the Rocky Mountains, where would she be safe? Certainly not in New York.

Then it occurred to her that if Mark wanted to scare her into not getting on that plane tomorrow evening, this was an effective way to do it. He couldn't be that deceptive and calculating, though. Surely.

"What, exactly, did these guys look like?" she asked.

"Big, rough-looking types. I didn't get a very good look at them."

"What makes you so sure they were following you?"

"For starters, everyplace I went, I'd find one or two of them hanging around outside, trying to act nonchalant. And they were dressed funny. Sport coats, no ties. Didn't look like tourists or locals."

Arianna contemplated him. "Mark, you aren't putting me on, are you?"

"This is not a joking matter, Arianna."

That was definitely true. She sighed. "Nothing's easy, is it?"

"It appears they're going to make you work for your big break, sweetpea."

"Well, I'm not going to be intimidated. Nobody is taking this opportunity away from me. Not even a bunch of cold-blooded killers!"

Mark nodded. "Somehow I thought you'd say that."

"You know me well."

He toyed with the curls at the side of her face. "I liked last night a lot better than this morning," he said.

"Me, too."

"Really?"

"Couldn't you tell?"

He smiled. "I sort of had that impression."

"You had me humming, Mark Lindsay, and you know it." She gave him a big hug. "How about if I take you to dinner after we get home? The restaurant of your choice."

"As a thank-you gesture?"

"That and...well, to celebrate our friendship."

"Is that what we're calling it?"

"Do you have a better suggestion?" she asked.

"My suggestions seem to get short shrift," he replied. "So yes, I'll let you take me to dinner to celebrate our friendship. Beyond that, I'm not making any promises."

Arianna laughed, then she reached up, pulled his face down and kissed him on the mouth. "Fair enough."

Mark took her face in his hands and was about to kiss her back when the front door burst open and several hooded men rushed in. Arianna screamed. Mark pushed her around behind him and faced them.

"What in the hell do you think you're doing?" he yelled at them. "Who are you? What do you want?"

Without a word, three of the men advanced, forcing them into a corner. Arianna was petrified. Her hands were on Mark's back. The men inched closer, like a pack of wolves surrounding their prey.

Mark threw a punch at the closest man, knocking him away. Then, spinning, he threw a karate kick at the second man, catching him on the shoulder. But the third man lunged and was on him, driving Mark to the floor. As Arianna watched, horrified, the three men pounced, subduing Mark. A fourth man came over quickly, taking her by the arm. It had all happened so fast she was stunned, too terrified to speak.

She stared with horror at the masked faces of the intruders. There were five altogether. A burly man who appeared to be the leader came to where she stood in the grasp of his associate. All she could see of his face were two brown disks in the eyeholes of his mask.

"Where's the book, lady?"

Arianna glanced down at Mark, who was still on the floor, pinned by the men who'd overpowered him. Then she looked at the coffee table. The man's eyes followed hers.

"That it?" he said, stepping over and picking up the loose pile of typed pages. He riffled through them. "Hell, I didn't know Salie knew this many words." The accent was Eastern in flavor. New York or New Jersey. He glanced at Mark. "Get Jackie Chan to his feet, boys. Better cover him or he's likely to break somebody's arm."

The men lifted Mark to his feet. One of them produced a silver-plated automatic.

"You've got what you came for," Mark said. "Just take it and go."

The man gave him a stern look, his eyes flashing. "Who asked you, mack?"

"Arianna only started to read the thing this morning," Mark insisted. "She doesn't even know what's in it yet."

The man looked at the pages more closely. "Yeah, well, who made all these notes along the edge?" He shook his head with disgust. "Just button it, pal, and let me ask the questions." Putting down the manuscript, he went over and stood in front of Arianna. "So what else did Sal give you, sweetheart?"

The man holding her arm tightened his grip. Her stomach clenched. "Just the manuscript."

"What about documents?"

"No, nothing like that, no," she replied. "Only what you see."

The man holding her smacked his gum. "Boss, maybe if we dunk her head in the toilet a few times she'll remember more."

"Maybe later," the head man said, dismissing the suggestion. "Take the two lovebirds in back someplace and make sure they don't fly the coop." He gave them both a piercing glare. "Meanwhile you two be thinking what else you can tell me that I'd find interesting while I look at this crap and decide what I'm going to do with you."

The men started to lead them off but the boss stopped them. "One last thing. The happier you make me, the nicer I'll be. Make me mad, and you can kiss your butt goodbye." His eyes appeared to smile and he waved them off.

As they were led past him, Arianna noticed a tattoo on the back of the man's hand. It was the Marine Corps emblem—a combination of an American eagle, a globe and an anchor. She was familiar with it because a guy she dated in college had been in the Marine Corps and had a tattoo like it on his shoulder.

The men took them to Mark's room. One produced some lengths of rope from his jacket pocket. They were told to put their hands behind their backs and were promptly bound. Then they were made to sit on the bed and their ankles were tied. Their legs were lifted onto the bed so that they lay side by side, facing each other.

"You two comfy?" one of the men said.

"Maybe they'd like pillows," another said.

"Or a rubber."

They all laughed and filed from the room. "Sleep tight," one said as a parting shot.

Realizing her first feelings of desperation, Arianna looked forlornly into Mark's eyes. "I'm so sorry," she said, choking back a sob.

"If anyone's to blame, it's me. I obviously wasn't careful enough."

"Don't blame yourself. You tried to warn me but I wouldn't listen."

"Let's don't dwell on that," he said, sounding resigned.

"Oh, Mark, do you think they'll kill us?" She could barely say the words, disbelieving this was actually happening. It was like a nightmare. Mark had talked about the danger, but she hadn't pictured it as graphic and terrifying as this.

"No. If they came with that intent, they wouldn't have worn masks. The dead can't make identifications."

That made sense. She felt a little better. "I hope you're right."

"But I think our best bet is to cooperate. Judging by their questions, they're as interested in Corsi's supporting documentation as in the manuscript. Where's the paper with the information on the mail drop?"

Arianna had to stop and think. She'd discovered it

during the drive from Aspen to Vail. What had she done with it? Then she remembered. She'd stuck it in the pouch on the door panel of the rental car. When she told Mark, he looked relieved.

"It's just as well. If they don't find everything they're after right away, it may buy us some time. If they come back demanding information about the documents, stall them," he said.

"What if they start torturing us?"

"Well, stall as long as you can."

"Why? What difference does it make?"

He hesitated. "I've got a plan, sweetpea."

"A plan? For what?"

"Escape."

"How?"

"The details are unimportant, but I'll need your help."

She gave him a skeptical look. What could he be thinking? They were tied up and unable to move. He needed the help of a SWAT team, not her.

"Listen, Arianna," he said, his tone surprisingly solemn. "This is going to sound strange but I've got a homing beacon mounted inside my watch. Tied up like this, I can't reach it, but if we roll over so that we're back-to-back, you might be able to activate it."

She blinked. "Mark, what in the world are you talking about?"

"Getting out of here," he said. "I tell you, we can summon help if you can activate the beacon. They jumped us so quickly, once they had a hold of my arms, there was nothing I could do."

Arianna wondered if he was in some kind of daze. "I

think the excitement has gotten to you. Just try to re-lax."

"Arianna," he said insistently, "I'm not joking. I have a homing beacon to use in emergencies. It's to let me summon help."

"Help from *whom?*"

"It doesn't matter."

"What do you mean, it doesn't matter?"

"My concern," he said, ignoring her reply, "is the distance and the mountains. I'm not sure the signal will get through."

She had a terrible sinking feeling. Mark had cracked up. On top of everything else, he'd flipped out. "Mark, honey, I know you're anxious, but I promise you we're going to be fine. I'll tell those men where the slip of paper is and then I'm sure they'll let us go."

"Listen, Arianna," he said, his voice just short of anger. "Those men are dangerous and we may not have very long. Will you please turn over so that your back is to me? This is no time for a debate!"

Arianna heard something in his tone, an edge, a firmness, that wasn't at all like him—certainly not the Mark of old, but maybe not even the new, cavalier Mark she'd found so alluring. True, they'd been over-whelmed by the intruders, but Mark had put up a good fight. It had taken three men to subdue him. And that karate kick had really surprised her.

"When did you get into martial arts?" she asked abruptly.

"Arianna, this is no time for questions."

"Well, I want to know. You never told me you could

do things like that. Surely you didn't pick up karate watching movies."

"No, I've had some training."

"When? What for?"

"Look," he said, losing his patience, "we can discuss this later. Turn over and activate the beacon on my watch before it's too late."

She sighed and flipped onto her other side. Mark did the same and scooted back against her so that their hands touched.

"First you're going to have to find my watch," he said.

"God, my wrists are tied so tight they're numb. I'm lucky I can move my fingers."

"You're going to have to do it."

Arianna had to scoot a bit higher on the bed. She found the ropes without any trouble, but had to dig down to get to his watch. "Okay," she said. "I feel the crystal."

"All right," he said. "On the side toward my fingers there are two knobs. The lower one, the one toward my thumb, is the one you have to find."

"Which way is your thumb?"

"I don't know. I guess you're going to have to feel."

"Oh, great." She felt around, but had such little range of motion that it was hard to find anything. But then the tip of her index finger come up against something. "I think I've found a knob," she said excitedly.

"Can you feel the other one?"

"No." She moved her fingers as best she could. "Yeah, here it is." Everything seemed upside down and backward. "Damn," she said. "This is impossible."

"No, it isn't. We've almost got it."

Suddenly the bedroom door opened and one of the men came in. He peered down at them lying back-to-back. "What happened? You two have a fight?"

"It's his breath," she said dryly.

"Sure you aren't trying to escape?"

"I can't even move my little finger," she retorted. "You tied me so tight I'm going to get gangrene. And believe me, if I do, I'll sue."

The man laughed.

"She's not kidding," Mark interjected.

"Well," the gangster said, "have your lawyer talk to our lawyer. Meanwhile, be thinking about those documents. The boss is getting impatient."

To their relief, he went out the door.

"Thank God," Arianna said.

She immediately began trying to find Mark's watch. This time she was able to locate the knobs more quickly. "All right, I think I know which one," she said.

"Turn it counterclockwise until it stops. It should only be one full turn or so."

"Counterclockwise? Mark, in this position, I don't know up from down, left from right."

"Just turn it backward. Your thumb-side down."

She groaned and gave the knob a turn, continuing until it wouldn't turn anymore. "There," she said. "I did it."

"This could get you the Medal of Honor," he said.

"I'd settle for a day of shopping."

"All the same, well done. Now all we can do is hope the signal got through."

Mark gripped her fingers. His touch was reassuring. Amid their struggle to activate the beacon, the immediacy of the danger had faded a bit into the background. But now, the helplessness she felt brought the urgency of their situation back to the forefront.

"Do you think we'll be all right?" she asked, her voice trembling.

"I hope so, darling. It all depends upon whether our signal got through."

He said it with such assurance, as if he really knew what he was doing.

"Mark," she said after a while, "please tell me what's going on."

"I'm hoping that help is on the way."

"But what help, who?"

He was silent.

"Mark?" She could feel him struggling as he turned over.

"Arianna," he said, "turn and face me."

She complied, finding him staring at her intently. "What?" she said.

"Have I ever let you down?"

She wondered what he was getting at. "No, I guess not."

"Well, I don't intend to now. You've got to trust me, that's all."

"But why can't you tell me?"

He didn't respond.

"Is it the police? Did you warn them that the Mafia

might show up here? Is that what you've been doing the past few days?"

Still he didn't answer. Arianna realized that was exactly what it was. Mark had gone to the police behind her back and he was too embarrassed to say so. Oh, God, she thought. If that were only true! How could he think she'd be upset with him under the circumstances? His paternalism could end up saving their lives!

"Look, don't worry about going behind my back," she said. "If I'd found out, I'd probably be mad as hell about you interfering in my work. I can't deny it. But it turns out you knew best," she said, her eyes glistening with emotion.

"We aren't out of this yet, Arianna. I just hope we'll have an opportunity to laugh about this later."

"As long as you know I'm glad you took charge," she said. "I promise never to give you a hard time about it. You were right and I was wrong. I admit it. A person should own up to it when they've made a mistake. It's only fair."

Mark smiled. Arianna gave him a quizzical look.

"Did I say something funny?" she asked.

"I don't know, it just struck me as odd that we're discussing the rules of our relationship and it's not clear whether an hour from now we'll be alive or dead."

"Or that we'll have a relationship at all," she added.

"That, too."

She gazed into his eyes, hating it that they were tied up. And all because of her damn stubbornness. She knew that now. "Oh, Mark, I am so sorry. It was selfish of me to think of my career, my wants, first. If we'd contacted the FBI like you wanted, this never would have happened."

Mark stretched his neck forward, bringing his face close enough to hers that he was able to kiss her lips. Tears filled her eyes.

"I'm doing my best to save you," he murmured. "I won't let anything happen to you. I promise."

A tear ran down her cheek and into her hair. Arianna squirmed forward, moving as close to him as she could. She kissed his chin. "Thank you for being the person you are," she whispered.

He reached his face out again and kissed her on the tip of the nose. "I love you, Arianna," he said.

Her eyes glistened. "Why did this have to happen just as things were starting to get better," she lamented.

"Suppose we could talk them into untying us for just half an hour?"

"It's not funny. I'm really scared."

"Let's hope the beacon works then. It may be our only chance," he said darkly.

7

EVERY TEN or fifteen minutes one of the men came into the bedroom to check on them, though they never said a word. And since there was no sign of the police, Arianna was beginning to fear that Mark's beacon hadn't worked.

"Where are your friends?" she whispered.

"I don't know, but it's too soon to give up hope. They have a long way to come."

That gave her pause. The police would be in Vail. Where were Mark's friends coming from, if not there? Denver? Washington, D.C.? If so, they weren't cops.

"Mark, who's coming? The FBI?"

He sighed, clearly not liking her questions.

"Why are you being so secretive?" she demanded.

"Arianna, sometimes it's better not to ask."

She blinked. What was wrong with him? Was he delusional, after all? Perhaps she'd been too quick to assume his plan was legitimate. But before she could question him further, two of the gangsters entered the room.

"Okay, lady," one of them said. "It's time to sing."

The men, both of whom were large, took her by the shoulders and lifted her from the bed. As they proceeded to untie her, Arianna's heart pounded. She rubbed her numb wrists, looked at Mark and wondered if this was the last time she would ever see him.

"What are you doing with her?" he demanded.

"Zip it," one of the men replied, dismissing him.

One gangster started for the door. The other gripped her arm and led her to the front room where the leader, the man with the tattoo on his hand, sat on the sofa with Sal Corsi's manuscript spread out on the coffee table before him. Arianna couldn't read his expression because he still wore the hood, but his body language indicated impatience.

"Sit down," he said, pointing to the chair opposite.

She was shoved in the direction of the chair and she dropped into it, rubbing her wrists. She glanced at the hooded men surrounding her, fighting her terror.

"Looks like when Salie spills his guts, he really spills them," the man said with disgust. "What do you got beside this manuscript?"

"Nothing," she replied, her voice trembling. "That's it."

"Yeah, well, Sal's hiding a load of documents somewhere and I've got to have them."

This was the moment of truth. Did she blurt out what she knew about the mail drop or try to lie her way past it? Her natural instinct was to resist. Earlier, Mark had said she should stall, so that's what she decided to do.

"What on earth makes you think I would know? I'm just a book editor."

He grunted. "Because if you're going to publish this book, you'd want proof that what Salie says is on the up-and-up. Nobody wants a lawsuit. You know that and Salie knew it, too. So, where are they?"

"I don't have them."

He pointed his finger accusingly. "I'm not asking you again."

Arianna's fear was tempered by her growing anger. She hated it when men tried to push her around. "Look, I'd like to see those documents as badly as you do."

The man shook his head. "Your ears don't work so good, do they?" He turned to his cohorts. "Which of you boys is ready to dunk the broad's head in the toilet?"

"Me, boss," one said.

"Okay," the head man said. "Go do your thing."

Arianna was horrified. One of the men stepped forward and grabbed her by the arm. "Wait," she protested. "All I said was that I'd like to see them as much as you. I didn't say I didn't know how to find them."

"Let's have it then," the leader said. "Where are they?"

The man let go of her and she sank back into the chair, her head bowed, hating that she'd been defeated. "They're in a mail drop in Brooklyn."

"Not good enough, sweetheart. You gotta be specific."

"I forget the address," she said, "but it's on a slip of paper in Mark's car."

"Does your boyfriend have the keys?"

"I believe so."

He signaled one of the men. "Get 'em."

The man went into the bedroom and returned a moment later with Mark's keys. Jingling them, he left the chalet. Silence settled over the room.

"What are you going to do with us?" Arianna asked, summoning her courage.

"I haven't decided," the spokesman said.

"We can't do you any harm," she volunteered. "We don't know what you look like...and I've been cooperative."

"You've been a pain in the butt." He pointed to one of his men. "Tie the broad up and take her to her boyfriend. If I see her again, it'll be to administer last rites."

That brought a chuckle from his friends.

Arianna breathed a sigh of relief. For the moment, at least, the gangsters weren't going to harm them. Now if Mark's friends would just show up, they might get out of this alive. Assuming Mark really had friends, of course.

When she entered the bedroom, Mark appeared relieved to see her. They tied her up and plunked her back on the bed like a sack of potatoes, then they left. Arianna turned her head toward Mark.

"They made me tell them about the mail drop," she lamented. "One of them went to get the slip of paper."

"That's all right, sweetpea, you did the best you could."

"I thought if I stalled long enough the police or the FBI or whoever we signaled would show up."

"Maybe they didn't get the message."

The words were no sooner out of his mouth when they heard the sound of an engine. It sounded like an airplane at first, then the distinctive throb of a helicopter became clear. They listened as the noise got louder.

"That could be them!" Mark said, sounding upbeat.

"You mean, we're being rescued?"

"I hope so."

It sounded as though the helicopter might be circling. There were shouts from the front room. They could hear the sound of a second aircraft and maybe a third. Then they heard a loud popping sound.

"Gunfire," Mark said grimly.

"Oh my God," Arianna gasped.

The shooting went on for several moments, interspersed with more shouts and the roar of helicopter engines. A couple of times they heard screams—men crying out with pain. After a time the shooting died down and the helicopters retreated into the distance. Then there was an eerie silence.

"Mark?" she said. "What's happening?"

"Shh," he said. "Listen!"

They were both quiet. The sound of the helicopter engines was distant now, faint. After a time it stopped. The wind moaned softly in the pines. The incongruous twitter of birds drifted through the air. Arianna swallowed hard, not knowing what had happened. Mark continued to listen.

They heard the sound of the front door flying open. Shots rang out and there was the clatter of booted feet on the hardwood floors. Arianna stopped breathing. She tensed.

Next, the bedroom door swung open so forcefully that the wall shook. Arianna cried out at the sight of a large man in combat fatigues and a flak jacket, carrying an automatic rifle. His face was smeared with green and brown paint, his eyes round as he stared at them.

"We're alone," Mark shouted to him. "It's okay."

"Mr. Lindsay?"

"Yes."

The man relaxed slightly, though he nervously fingered the forearm of his weapon. "They're in here!" he shouted over his shoulder to unseen companions.

A second man, similarly attired and also carrying an automatic rifle, appeared. His stern expression softened some at the sight of them. "How many of them were there?" he asked, his question clearly addressed to Mark.

"Five."

"We've got them all then." He left the room and the first man lowered his weapon, letting it hang at his side.

"How about untying us," Mark said.

"Sure. Sorry, sir."

The man leaned his rifle against the wall, took a knife from a sheath on his belt and stepped to the bed. First he cut Arianna's bonds, then Mark's. "You all right, ma'am?" he asked as she sat up on the edge of the bed.

"Yes," she said. "Thanks to you." She glanced at Mark, who came around the bed. "And Mark, of course."

Mark put his arm around her shoulders. She clutched his waist, trembling. She was so stunned no words came to her. Even her feelings were confused, though there was a measure of relief.

They heard voices in the front room.

"They're in here, sir," came a voice moments before an older, balding man in khaki pants and a blue windbreaker appeared. He was followed by the second man they'd seen. "Ah, Mark," he said with a smile. "Good to see you in one piece."

They shook hands.

"It's good to be in one piece, believe me," Mark replied. "This is Arianna Hamilton, by the way."

"Ah, yes," the older man replied. "The young lady. How do you do, Miss Hamilton?"

"Hello," she said, taking his proffered hand.

"I'm Mr. Jones," he said. The corner of his mouth curled slightly. "You seem to be in good health. Happy to see we arrived in time."

"Not as glad as I am, believe me," she said.

The man turned his attention back to Mark. "I believe it would be prudent to leave right away."

"Check."

"Fortunately the cabin's isolated and the nearby structures don't seem to be occupied at the moment."

"Yes, that's my impression," Mark said. "But no telling when someone might happen along."

Arianna was a bit taken aback by Mark's easy familiarity with Mr. Jones, but she said nothing as they went into the front room. There were bodies on the floor— two of their captors. Both wore ski masks, their torsos soaked with blood. Three other men in fatigues and camouflage paint were in the room. One was covering the body nearest the door with a sheet of plastic. Arianna quailed at the sight. Mark and Jones hurried her out the door.

"Where are the others?" Mark asked as they stepped out into the fresh mountain air. He had hold of Arianna's hand.

"Two are in the woods behind the cabin and one down at the parking lot. That body's already been removed," Jones said. "We'll have the others out of here in no time."

"Was much damage done to the building?" Mark asked, turning and peering up at the facade.

"No. I think the biggest task will be cleaning up inside, but we'll get right on it."

"Check for bullet holes," Mark said. "Patch what you can. Maybe we can pass off any others the owners spot as errant rounds from hunters."

"Sounds plausible," Jones agreed.

Arianna had been listening with growing amazement. Mark almost sounded as though he was part of the operation. And she sensed a deference being shown to him. He couldn't possibly have developed this kind of familiarity with the local police, or for that matter, the FBI.

"I don't anticipate any trouble from the local authorities," Jones was saying. "But we can control only so much. It would be best if we tidy up and get the hell out of here."

"Roger that," Mark said.

Arianna gave him a disbelieving look. *Roger that?* What did Mark think he was, some kind of honorary Green Beret? "Mark," she said, taking his arm.

"Just a second, sweetpea," he said, cutting her off. "I need to talk to Mr. Jones. Will you be all right for a moment or two?"

"Sure," she said, realizing she had no choice.

As she watched, Mark and the man went off about twenty yards from her. They were deep in conversation, and their obvious familiarity confounded her. She watched the paramilitary troops as they moved around the property. They were not behaving at all like police, so she doubted now that they were some sort of elite SWAT team, as she'd first imagined. In fact, they wore no insignia or other identifying marks on their uniforms.

Mark and Jones were still in the midst of an animated conversation when she heard a chopper in the distance. Then, over the tops of the trees in the direction of the chalet parking lot, she saw a helicopter rise and head in the direction of Vail. It was so far away that she couldn't get a good look at it, but her impression was that it was not military.

After another minute, Mark made his way back toward her as Jones conferred with one of his men. Judging by Mark's expression, he wasn't exactly pleased, but he did seem more at ease than during their ordeal.

"Mark," she said when he came up to her. "What's going on?"

"Mr. Jones and I have decided to leave immediately. I told him you'd want your things. Do you mind if I pack everything for you? It's a little messy inside."

She took a long deep breath. "Who are these people, Mark? They aren't police."

"No, that's true."

"Then who are they?"

"Arianna," he said, taking her hand, "let's discuss this later. Right now we have to get out of here. It's very important."

She was utterly taken aback by his reaction.

"Here, sit down on the steps," he said. "I'll be back

in a couple of minutes and I promise you everything will be all right."

Arianna did as he asked, but she was certain now something very weird was going on. Then she remembered. "Oh, Mark," she called after him.

He'd just stepped inside, and stuck his head back out the door. "What?"

"The manuscript. I can't leave it."

A dark look came over his face. "Okay."

He was gone about five minutes. While she waited, Arianna observed Mr. Jones, who kept away from her. His men came to where he was standing and conferred with him a couple of times, but mostly he observed things from a distance, though he did check his watch a number of times.

When Mark reappeared, one of the men was with him, carrying their suitcases. Mark handed her a paper sack. Peering inside, she saw it was the loosely stacked manuscript, the sheets thrown together haphazardly.

"We've got to go," he said, taking their suitcases from the man.

She walked with him to where Mr. Jones waited.

"All set?" the man said amiably, though he glanced at his watch as he spoke.

They headed toward the parking lot. As they walked, Arianna shot Mark several glances, but he pretended he didn't notice. When they were almost there, she couldn't contain herself any longer.

"The shoot-out is going to be covered up, isn't it?" she said. "You're not going to report it and you're going to pretend it never happened."

"Arianna, please," Mark said impatiently. "We'll discuss it later."

"I don't like being a party to this," she warned.

"You're not a party to it, Miss Hamilton," Jones said, glancing at her. "It never happened."

"What do you mean, it never happened?" Despite her best intentions, there was an edge in her voice. "We were kidnapped by mobsters and you killed them trying to rescue us. They may not have been nice people, but they *are* dead and that can't be ignored."

"Believe me," Jones said, "it's easier if you think of it as a bad dream. No one innocent was hurt and that's all that matters."

Arianna was aghast. Even more distressing was Mark's apparent complicity. Taking his arm and drawing him back so that Jones couldn't hear, she said in a low voice, "What the hell is happening? You know we can't leave the scene of a crime. We have to do something."

"I am doing something, Arianna. I'm getting you out of here."

"Well, you are also making me an accessory to a crime. Come on, Mark, you can't just expect me to waltz off as if nothing happened."

"Arianna, I said we'd talk at the right time. And *this* is not the right time. Now, please, the fact that you've been involved in the operation is bad enough."

She was shocked. His voice was sterner than she'd ever heard it. Was this the man she thought she knew? Whatever this charade was, he hadn't just fallen into it over the last couple of days. He was a part of it.

When they arrived at the parking area, they found

two more helicopters—a large one and a small one—and several armed men. The aircraft seemed to be commercial rather than military, but the identifying insignia had been painted over. They walked directly toward the smaller chopper.

"Mark," she said, taking him by the arm again and stopping him. "What about that slip of paper, the one with the address of the mail drop?"

He reacted with mild annoyance, though he said nothing to her. "Mr. Jones," he called to the other man. "Where's the slip of paper from my car? The gangster you got in the parking lot should've had it on him."

Jones produced a piece of paper from his jacket pocket and handed it to Mark, who in turn handed it to Arianna. She put it in the sack with the manuscript.

"That all?" Jones said.

Mark looked at her. "Anything else?"

"No." Under her breath, she added, "But I'd be happier if I knew what was going on."

If Mark heard, he ignored her.

Once at the chopper, Mark helped her climb aboard, then tossed their bags in before settling down next to her in the rear passenger seat. Jones had stepped aside to speak to one of his lieutenants, then he, too, got in, sitting by the pilot. After giving the pilot instructions, Jones settled back in his seat. The engine came to life. In moments they were airborne, the mountainside dropping away below them.

Arianna glanced at Mark. "Where are we going? Or is it top-secret?"

He gave her a crooked smile. "It's top-secret." But as he said it, he took her hand, squeezing it affectionately.

She gazed down at his fingers, wondering who they belonged to—certainly not the Mark Lindsay she'd known. In fact, she was no longer sure she knew him at all. The man who'd come to Aspen wasn't the one she'd known in New York. And this one, the one mixed up with these mysterious people, was even more confounding. It was as though he'd just removed a mask, exposing a whole new person, one who was completely alien and unfamiliar.

As they flew over the peaks, her mind went over the past few harrowing hours. The kidnapping, the beacon signal and now their dramatic rescue. It was like a dream. Or a bad movie.

Mark had promised to explain what was going on, but for now he seemed content to hold her hand. She gave him another appraising look, thoroughly intrigued. One thing was certain. This wasn't the man she'd been engaged to.

She looked out the window again, and watched the sun. Judging by its location, they were headed in a southern or southeastern direction.

"Mark, are we going back to Aspen?"

He nodded. "Yeah."

"Why?"

"It's the closest suitable airport."

She waited for further explanation, but none was forthcoming. "So, are you taking me back to Zara's?"

"No," he replied.

"Then where?"

"You'll see."

Arianna bit her lip. She didn't like what was happening, but she knew she was not in a position to complain. He'd saved her from the Mob, after all. Still...

"Can't you even give me a hint?"

He rolled his eyes. "There's an executive aircraft waiting for us there. It will take us to a safe location where we'll have time to sit down and sort this all out."

He was being firm and it frustrated her. Mark seemed to notice she was unhappy.

"I realize this is all very confusing," he said, "but there's no way to avoid that at the moment. I've promised that at the proper time I'll explain and I will. For now you'll have to trust me."

That, she realized, was easier said than done.

8

As THE CROW FLIES, the distance between Vail and Aspen was not that great. It was simply a matter of crossing over a mountain range, and by helicopter it was a piece of cake. Seeing Aspen by air, the relative familiarity was a relief. Arianna was eager to get on the ground.

The chopper landed at a remote corner of the airfield, away from the terminal building, which did not please her. Looking out, she saw an executive aircraft parked nearby, its passenger door open and boarding ladder down. Arianna could see that they intended to take her right from the helicopter to the plane. There would be no buying a magazine at the airport newsstand.

Jones got out, followed by Mark, who waited to help her. Arianna stepped down, clutching the sack with the manuscript to her chest.

"That's our plane," Mark said unnecessarily.

"Yes, but I'm not getting on it until I get the whole story."

Mark glanced at Jones, who was headed for the plane, then consulted his watch impatiently. "Can't I tell you when we're aboard?"

"No, it's now or never."

"Why?"

"Because if I don't like what I hear, I'm leaving. I'm getting off at this stop."

Mark sighed woefully. "I knew that one day I'd have to face this," he said. "I just never pictured it standing on the tarmac in Aspen, Colorado."

His words made her stomach drop. A chilling realization went through her. She was about to discover she didn't know the real Mark Lindsay at all.

"Coming?" Jones called to them

"In a minute," Mark replied. "Go ahead and get aboard." He turned back to her, obviously anguishing as he tried to figure out how to express himself.

Arianna decided to beat him to the punch. "You aren't the man I was engaged to, are you, Mark?"

"Of course I am. There's just a little more to the story, that's all." He drew a deep breath and stared off at Snowmass Mountain. "For several years I've been involved with a clandestine organization that does...let's say, extremely sensitive work. It's a top-secret government agency."

"Oh my God," she said, her jaw going slack. "You're a spy?"

"Let's say operative. That's more precise."

She felt her heart skip a beat. She almost forgot to breathe. "Mark Lindsay, I was supposed to marry you and you're just now telling me you're James Bond?"

He shrugged. "Well, we didn't get married, did we?"

"No, but we were *going* to!"

"Close only counts in horseshoes and hand grenades, sweetpea."

"But what if we *had* married?" Her eyes narrowed

and she forced herself to take a deep breath. "Tell me the truth. Would you have told me before we got married, or were you going to swear me to secrecy on our wedding night?"

"Of course I was going to tell you before the wedding, Ari."

"I don't know whether to believe you or not. Based on what I've seen today, it's just as likely you'd have let me find out by accident. I can see it now—I'd be looking through your underwear drawer and find your code book. Or maybe a Superman suit."

He laughed. "I draw the line at leaping tall buildings in a single bound. You know heights bother me."

"Yeah, well, apparently deception and duplicity don't."

Mark glanced impatiently toward the plane. "Arianna, I hadn't intended for it to come out this way, but dammit, those guys were serious. I didn't have a choice. And it did save you, don't forget. I'd like it if you were a little more appreciative of that fact."

"I am appreciative. But my point is, you aren't the person you represented yourself to be. Don't you see what a betrayal it was? I thought I was engaged to Clark Kent, but you're really...Super Agent!"

"It's a little more prosaic than that, I assure you. So now that you know the truth, can we go?"

"No, not until you answer one more question. And I want the truth. Who do you spy for? Is it our side?"

"Yes."

"The CIA?"

"No comment."

Her eyes narrowed. "Are you loving this...not being able to tell me anything?"

"Come on," he said. "I answered your question. We're leaving. Now. Whether you want to face up to it or not, you could have been killed. Next time there might be ten of them. I can't call on the Marine Corps to rescue you, but I can take you where you'll be safe."

She rolled her eyes, utterly frustrated. "What happened to that nice, accommodating, solicitous man I was engaged to?"

"You broke up with him," he said dryly.

Arianna wasn't sure who this Mark Lindsay was, but the man she'd been engaged to had to be in there somewhere. Until he gave her a darn good reason not to, she'd do as he asked. Besides, what alternative did she have? "All right, Batman," she said, resigned. "Take me to your cave."

He chuckled, genuinely amused.

"Mark," she said, suddenly wary. "It isn't really a cave, is it?"

He laughed again. But he didn't answer her.

THEY HAD BEEN AIRBORNE for twenty minutes before Arianna managed to relax. Everything had happened so quickly that her emotions hadn't kept up. Mark, who was seated beside her, had been quiet, probably having a bit of trouble coming down himself. Mr. Jones, whose name, she was sure, was no more Jones than the man in the moon, sat directly behind the pilot. She and Mark were in the rear. Surprisingly, there was a flight attendant aboard, a pretty young Japanese woman whose English was nearly flawless. She didn't wear a uniform, just a plain gray skirt and white silk blouse.

"May I bring you something to drink, Miss Hamilton?" she asked solicitously.

"Maybe some water," Arianna said. "Please."

"Mr. Lindsay?" the young woman said, turning to him.

"Nothing, thanks."

The attendant nodded graciously and withdrew.

Arianna reached down and took Mark's hand, which seemed to surprise him, but he also acted pleased. Now that the adrenaline had stopped flowing, she was a little shaky and wanted reassurance. Worse, she felt guilty about all the trouble she'd caused. Her obsession with the manuscript was the problem. If she'd listened to Mark and sent it to the FBI, none of this would have happened. Those men wouldn't have been killed, and her life wouldn't be in danger.

A well of emotion gripped her and her eyes started to bubble. She wiped away the tears that began running down her cheeks. Mark noticed.

"Hey, sweetpea, what's the matter?"

"Oh, Mark, I feel so badly about all the trouble I caused."

"It's not your fault."

"Of course it is. I was being selfish about Sal Corsi's book. I didn't think about anyone else, even you. I haven't fully appreciated it until now, but you were right when you said I was single-minded when it came to my work."

The attendant brought her a glass of sparkling mineral water. Arianna thanked her and took the glass, sipping from it.

"I know I haven't been a very nice person," she said. "And my enlightenment has come at a price. A terrible price when you consider the lives of those men."

"They weren't exactly model citizens, Arianna."

"No, but they were human beings. And what about Sal Corsi?"

"You can't blame yourself for that. You never even met him."

"Yeah, but if I'd handled things differently from the beginning, he might not have died. And what about Zara, my own sister?"

"Hey," Mark said. "I think you're taking this a little too far. It's good you've learned a lesson, but you can't take all the sins of the world on your shoulders."

"You really don't resent me, Mark?"

"Of course not."

"What if this creates problems for you…in your work?" she said, glancing toward Jones.

"You can help me by cooperating," he said. "You'll be a bit of an inconvenience, I grant you, but as far as I'm concerned, it's well worth it."

"Do you mean that?"

"Definitely. If that weren't true, I wouldn't have gone to all the trouble to be sure you're safe."

She squeezed his arm and lay her head against his shoulder. To her relief, she'd discovered that the new Mark—the spy—still had some of the good qualities of the old Mark. He was caring, thoughtful.

But that made her consider the other faces of Mark Lindsay she'd seen the past few days. The man who'd come to her in Aspen had shown her a new side, as well, a side she hadn't seen before—he had been suave, playful. In Vail, she'd seen yet another side of him, an elusive side that intrigued her.

And now, well, she'd discovered that Mark was James Bond. She hadn't quite figured out what to do with this one yet. It made her wonder, though, how many other surprises were in store for her.

For the first time in years, Arianna doubted herself. How could she have been engaged to Mark and not seen any of it? *Not a hint.* Was that his fault, or hers? Maybe he hadn't been entirely open and forthcoming, but the evidence had to be there. She had simply missed it. Blind, self-centered, selfish. That's what she'd been. In fact, it was a miracle that Mark had any compassion for her at all. Maybe she was lucky. Maybe fate was giving her another chance.

SOMEHOW SHE'D MANAGED to fall asleep, and when she awoke she was still on the plane. Mark had moved a few seats away and was chatting with the flight attendant. A pang of jealousy shot through her. She knew now that Mark had been living a double life. Could that have included other women? Arianna realized she was being paranoid, probably as a result of having had her legs knocked out from under her.

The attendant noticed she was awake and immediately got up, coming to her.

"Good, you're awake," she said. "We'll be landing shortly. Is there anything you'd like? Another glass of water? Something to nibble on?"

"No, I'm fine," Arianna told her, stretching. "Thank

you." She glanced out the window and saw that dusk was rapidly falling. "Where are we?"

"I don't know," the young woman replied. "You'll have to ask Mr. Lindsay."

Of course, it wasn't true—the woman was giving her the party line. As she moved away, Mark returned to the seat beside Arianna. She gave him a thin smile. "Pretty girl. Been on many missions with her?"

Mark chuckled. "No. As a matter of fact, I met her today for the first time."

"Must be the allure of a man with deep, dark secrets," she said.

"Do you find my deep, dark secrets alluring?"

"No comment," she replied, which brought a laugh from Mark. She looked out the window again. They were still at a fairly high altitude. She could see a few scattered lights on the darkening sepia landscape. "We're still in Oz, I see. Or flying over it, anyway."

"Were you hoping it was a dream?"

She regarded him. "I haven't decided yet."

"You'll feel better when we've landed and you've had a nice hot meal."

Arianna peered out the window a third time. "I'm sure you won't tell me where we are, but would it hurt if I know what country I'm in?"

"We're still in the States."

"Then I'm not going to be exchanged for a Soviet spy?"

"Hey, sweetpea, this is an airplane not a time machine," he said, taking her hand and giving it a squeeze.

"It wouldn't have surprised me if you told me it *was* a time machine. I hardly know what to trust anymore."

"I feel badly about that," he said. "I really want this to be a pleasant experience. I want you to feel safe and relaxed."

"How long are we going to stay wherever it is we're going?"

"I'm not sure yet. Several days, probably."

"Do I get a vote?"

"Yes, but after what happened the last couple of days, I will insist on a veto."

There was a time when Arianna would have taken exception to such a remark, but after the trouble she'd caused, she was hardly in a position to complain. "Whatever you say, 007."

Mark reached over and gently squeezed her shoulder. "I'm kind of liking this. Maybe I should have offered to show you my Bat Cave a long time ago."

She gave him a look. "You might be on a roll, Agent Lindsay, but I wouldn't push my luck, if I were you."

He grinned. "Thanks for the warning."

"A girl can't surrender all her dignity."

"Point taken."

Mark, she decided, seemed to have become lighter on his feet. Or maybe it was a matter of finally feeling free to be himself. Whatever it was, it seemed to be working and she certainly wasn't going to complain.

The flight attendant asked them to fasten their seat belts, and judging by the sounds and motion of the plane, Arianna decided they would be landing soon. She looked out at the dark landscape once more. To the west there remained enough color in the sky to silhouette the jagged line of the mountains, but other than a few scattered lights, there was little sign of life below. For all she knew, they could have been landing on the moon.

"Your hideout is out in the sticks, isn't it?" she said to Mark without turning from the window.

"Yup."

"Do you come here often?"

"No."

"If we'd married, would I have been able to come here?"

"No."

"Are you going to blindfold me until I'm in my cell?"

"Jones and I discussed that option," Mark said with a laugh, "but we decided against it."

Arianna glanced up the cabin at Mr. Jones, who'd kept to himself the entire trip. She was glad about that. There was something cold and unfeeling about the man. All she could see of him was his bald head over the seat back. He appeared to be reading files, just as he had earlier.

"So, is he Q?" she asked Mark.

"Not exactly. But if it helps, you can think of him that way. Whatever makes it easy for you."

She gazed into Mark's eyes. "I want to ask you something. If we'd married and I said I wanted you to resign, would you have done it?"

His expression turned sardonic. "But you didn't marry me, sweetpea, so the issue is moot."

The words flowed so easily, as if he had no idea how stunned she was by all this. She'd never thought about it before, but other women must have had this experience—when the mild-mannered man they thought they knew turned out to be a spy, it had to be a shock. So what was left that she could trust? If Mark had been able to deceive her about his true identity, what else had he kept hidden?

"Mark, do your parents know what you do?"

"I think it's better if we don't discuss that."

"But I want to know if I'm the only one who's been in the dark."

"My father is aware of bits and pieces, but that's all I'm going to say."

She gave him a hard look. "You're enjoying this. *Really* enjoying this. I know in my soul you are. And all this time I'd been under the illusion you were a nice guy who worked in the family banking business."

"You know what they say, honey. Never judge a book by its cover."

9

WHEN THE PLANE touched down, Arianna became, if anything, even more anxious. For one of the few times in her life, she felt utterly out of control, swept along by events that were beyond her. Mark had tried to put her at ease, but after the day she'd had, it was hard to feel confident about anything. Yet what alternative did she have?

The plane taxied from the runway, finally stopping in front of a small structure that could hardly be considered a terminal building. It did not have the look of a public facility, and she decided they'd landed at a private field. The Japanese flight attendant brought Arianna her paper sack with the manuscript, having stored it during the flight. Mr. Jones got to his feet and stretched. He looked back at her for the first time since boarding and offered a perfunctory smile.

Meanwhile, the door had been opened and a small boarding ladder was brought to the plane. The attendant, who stood at the opening, gestured for them to disembark. Jones went out first, then Arianna and Mark.

They were greeted by a biting, chilly breeze. She surmised that they were on a mountain plateau at a fairly high altitude. Judging by the direction and duration of the flight, she figured they were most likely in Montana.

As Jones walked slowly toward a nondescript sedan parked nearby, she stood on the tarmac, shivering and clutching her sack to her as she waited for Mark to say goodbye to the flight attendant. Once he was on the ground, he ushered her in the direction of the vehicle, putting his arm around her as they walked.

"You really don't know her?" Arianna said, unable to help herself.

"No."

"It would be all right if you do," she said. "Part of James Bond's charm for a woman is the knowledge that every other woman wants him, too."

"The line you have to join is fairly short," he said.

Arianna saw a tiny smile at the corner of his mouth. "False humility," she said under her breath, but loud enough for him to hear.

The driver of the waiting car was a middle-aged man and was not in uniform. Jones climbed in the front seat next to him. Mark opened the rear door for her and got in behind her. The driver started the engine and they proceeded across the tarmac and out a gate onto a paved road. There were no buildings in sight.

They hadn't gone far before Jones turned and looked over the seat at her. "I'd like to say a few things if I may, Miss Hamilton. We haven't been able to fully prepare for your visit, so you may find things a bit...let's say, improvised. We normally don't have guests."

"I can well imagine," she said.

"Every effort will be made to see that you're comfortable, but our facilities are designed for staff needs. It will be necessary to ask for your cooperation."

"Certainly, Mr. Jones. I'm obviously indebted to you."

He accepted her courtesy with equanimity. "I'm afraid I'll have to ask you to restrict your movement to your quarters, the lounge and cafeteria areas, unless you're in the company of a staff person. In other words, all but a small part of the facility will be off-limits to you. I assume that will not be an imposition."

"No, my grandmother always taught me to respect the rules of other people's homes."

Jones smiled as though not completely sure whether she'd intended politeness or sarcasm. "I'll also have to ask you not to engage any of the staff in conversation about their work or the facility—it creates a burden on them if you ask questions. Mr. Lindsay will be your sole source of information. The alternative is to isolate you, and Mr. Lindsay has assured me that would be unnecessary."

Arianna glanced at Mark. "I'm flattered by his confidence. And I promise, Mr. Jones, I won't do anything to let either him or you down."

"Excellent," he replied.

Mark took her hand and, drawing it to his mouth, kissed her fingers. It was a small thing, but she liked it.

They drove for approximately two or three miles until they approached a large dimly lit complex enclosed by a chain-link fence topped with coils of razor wire. It didn't exactly look like a prison, but the overall impression was close enough to make her quail. A large sign near the entrance had been covered with a tarp.

That struck her as odd—more because it was obviously a temporary measure than for any other reason.

She would have felt more uneasy if it hadn't been for Mark. He was calm and relaxed and she found herself drawing on his strength. That hadn't been a part of their relationship in the past and so felt a little strange now. Yet there was something about it that she liked.

The gate was guarded, but not by paramilitary troops. There were two uniformed men. That was rather low-profile security, she thought, considering the clandestine nature of the installation. On the other hand, perhaps being understated was important.

Arianna wondered what sort of work Mark actually did as an operative in an organization devoted to espionage. Was his banking background a total subterfuge? If so, were his real skills in cryptology, demolitions, electronic surveillance or some other sneaky line of work? It was incredible to think he could kill people with his bare hands. She could hardly fathom sleeping with a man for months on end, and being totally oblivious to his true nature. Yet that's exactly what had happened. She shivered at the notion.

There were a number of buildings scattered around the compound, most of them small. One or two looked as though they might house offices, but the rest were more of an industrial nature—shops or small storage facilities. The car proceeded to a building of the latter type, which made her wonder. Was this where the staff resided? If so, the accommodations were probably pretty basic.

What other new revelations would this night bring? she wondered. This was the first time she'd be sleeping under the same roof with Mark in his true persona. Now that the cat was out of the bag, would other layers of deception drop away? And if so, what would she discover?

They got out of the car, Arianna still clutching her manuscript. Odd, but it was almost as much a source of shame as it was a treasure. Since the kidnapping, it had become an afterthought—the reason they were there, but of secondary interest. And to think, poor Zara had had her vacation ruined because of the thing.

Or worse. She sent a silent prayer to her twin, wherever she was. She didn't know what she'd do if something awful had happened to her. Her hope now was that they would both survive to tell their tales the next time they saw each other.

Mr. Jones led them to a short flight of stairs leading up to a small concrete porch. The entrance was a set of double doors made of steel. There were no windows. Above the doors was a light with a metal shade that shook in the wind. Arianna shivered at the bleakness of the setting and hoped the inside would be more hospitable.

When Jones opened the heavy door, bright light spilled out. The interior was a bit more cheerful, though the overall mood was institutional. Carpets were scattered around the linoleum floor to give an impression of warmth. The furniture looked to be standard government issue. The lobby area was empty, but a couple of small offices surrounding it on three sides were occupied by men in civilian clothes. All but one or two appeared to be Asian.

On the fourth side of the room was a bank of elevators, which seemed odd considering it was a one-story building. Jones turned to them. "Excuse me a minute, please."

Arianna looked at Mark, whose stoic expression turned into a laconic smile as they exchanged glances. "You have to admit it's different," he said lightly.

"Well, it's not that elegant Manhattan office I've associated you with in the past."

"Being an adventurer has its price," he quipped.

Jones had gone into one of the offices where one of the men handed him something, which he put in his pocket. He returned to the reception area and headed to the elevator, gesturing for them to join him. Jones called a car by inserting a key and turning it. As they waited, the driver arrived with their bags.

"I'll take those," Mark said. "No need for you to carry them down."

The man nodded and Mark took the bags.

"Jack of all trades, I see," she said out of the corner of her mouth.

"These things happen when you work for the government."

They waited for the elevator. There was no floor indicator, but it was obvious the only direction they could go was down.

The car arrived and the three of them stepped inside. Again there was no floor indicator, only an up and down arrow.

"So," she said, breaking the silence, "we *are* going to the Bat Cave, after all."

"In a manner of speaking," Mark said with a small smile.

"I hope you aren't claustrophobic, Miss Hamilton," Jones said.

"I hope I'm not, too."

The elevator car hurtled into the bowls of the earth at what seemed to be at a high speed, though Arianna had no idea how far they were traveling. Finally it stopped and the doors slid open. The men waited for her to exit.

Arianna stepped out into a small reception area. There was more government issue–type furnishings. There were three sets of double doors on the other three sides of the anteroom. The set opposite them was closed, the other two were open. Beyond them stretched two long corridors. Mr. Jones pointed to the left.

"The cafeteria and recreation rooms, including a small library, are that way," he said. "The sleeping quarters are this way." He started walking through the doorway to the right and proceeded down the corridor. Mark and Arianna followed at a distance.

"Sometimes the company is more important than the accommodations," Mark said under his breath.

She slowed to allow Jones to get out of earshot. "What does that mean, that we're sharing a room?"

"It could be arranged."

"Let's have a look first. I'm sure the other *Lindsay* girls fall into your hands like ripe fruit, but I'm going to give my willpower a test."

"Challenges are nice."

The doors along the way were numbered, much like those in a hotel. One opened as they approached and a petite Asian woman exited. She wasn't as attractive as the flight attendant, and she was older. Seeing them, she smiled and bowed slightly, then moved along the hallway in the direction from which they'd come. Arianna glanced back at her. She was dressed simply in slacks and a blouse, her hair short-cropped.

"Is it my imagination, or are there a large number of Asians here?"

"I don't believe it's your imagination," Mark replied.

They came to a side corridor and Jones turned down it. There were only half a dozen doors spaced along its length. At the end was a wall painting of fighter jets flying in formation.

Jones stopped at the second to the last door on the left. He retrieved a room key from his pocket. "Miss Hamilton," he said, "this is your room." Pushing the door open, he flipped on a light switch inside and stepped back to allow her to enter.

Arianna went into the room. It was Spartan, but pleasant. A single bed, nightstand with lamp and telephone, a table and two chairs, a dresser and a TV. There were three lithographs on the walls—missiles of various types.

"Looks comfortable," she said, glancing around. "The phallic symbols are a nice touch."

Mark laughed. Jones managed a mild smile.

"That's the bathroom," Jones said, pointing toward the door in the corner.

"I'm not overly claustrophobic," Arianna said, "but out of curiosity, how many tons of rock will be over my head while I sleep?"

"We're about three hundred and fifty feet under-ground," Jones replied.

"Saves on the heating bill, I suppose."

"But not much of a view," Mark added.

"You must feel right at home, Batman."

Mark and Jones exchanged amused glances. Arianna went to the table and put down the sack that contained the manuscript. Jones followed her, handing her the room key.

"Are you hungry, Miss Hamilton? The cafeteria's closed, but I can arrange to have a meal brought to you."

She shook her head. "No, I really don't want any-thing."

"Are you sure, Arianna?" Mark asked. "We've hardly eaten today."

"I guess I lost my appetite in the excitement."

"We've got to keep up our strength." He turned to Jones. "Why don't you have somebody bring us a cou-ple of light meals, if you would?"

"Gladly." Then, addressing Arianna, he said, "The cafeteria opens at 6:00 a.m. and stays open for break-fast until nine-thirty. Feel free to go down at any time."

"Thank you."

"There's a coffee room adjacent to it where you can get soft drinks and snacks twenty-four hours a day. Feel free to help yourself."

"You're very hospitable."

Jones smiled, then, turning to Mark, he handed him another room key and proceeded to the door. "I'll say good-night. You've had a rough day and I'm sure you're both tired. Someone will be down with your meals shortly."

"Good-night."

Jones left the room, closing the door behind him. Arianna leaned against the table, staring at Mark. There was an unusual kind of electricity in the air.

"So," she said, "this is what it's like to be in the lair of a spy."

Mark went to the bed and sat down, bouncing a little. "I think I prefer my bed at home, to be honest. It would be bigger."

"The humility's a nice touch," she said, "but it's too late, Mark. The cat's already out of the bag."

He reflected on her remark. "I'm wondering if you aren't setting too high a standard for me," he said. "Keep talking like this and I might come down with a case of performance anxiety."

Arianna laughed. "Jones is barely out of the room and already we're talking sex. Did I somehow indicate I was ready to give good old 007 a whirl?"

"Must be all the missiles on the walls," he replied with mock seriousness.

"Of course, you're perfectly aware I'm bubbling over with questions."

"Questions are never a problem," he replied. "It's the answers I have to be concerned about."

"Spoken like a true secret agent."

Mark smiled.

"But seriously," she said, "do you do any of the real sneaky stuff?"

"Like what?"

"You know. Poison capsules, for example. When

you mentioned it this afternoon you were just kidding, right?"

"Yes."

Arianna walked across the room in front of him, knowing by the way he watched her that he was feeling the sexual energy. "Have you ever killed anyone?" she asked.

"No."

"Swear?"

"I swear."

She stopped to appraise him. "You'd probably deny it even if it was true."

"There's nothing I could say that would convince you beyond what I've said."

"So, which is better, that I assume you have or haven't?"

Mark pondered the question. "Let's go with haven't."

Arianna had no idea if it was true, but she liked that he'd said it, anyway.

"Is that your biggest worry?" he asked.

"No, there's another," she said, resuming her pacing. "Why did you want to marry me?"

"Isn't it obvious?"

"Not now."

"How so?"

"Well," she said, "for all I know, you just wanted a cover."

"If all I was looking for was a cover, I didn't have to shoot quite that high."

"Meaning?"

"Meaning, the real reason was because I loved you."

She searched his eyes, overcome by a well of anxiety.

"What's the matter, Arianna?"

She swallowed, the kidding and swagger of only a moment before forgotten. "I'm having trouble computing that the mild-mannered investment banker I almost married is a spy. Tell me this is a dream, Mark. A joke. Something."

"I'm not a spy."

"All right, an operative."

His expression was serious at first, but then a smile crept over his face. "Come here," he said, holding out his hand.

Arianna moved toward him tentatively, stopping in front of him. He took her hand in his and toyed affectionately with her fingers.

"I'd like you to believe that all this doesn't have any effect on my feelings for you," he said softly. "They are the same as they've always been."

"But don't you see, Mark, you're a completely different person than I thought. By definition, it's impossible for me to see you in the same light."

"Well, which me do you like better?"

She bit her lip. "I'm not sure."

"Oh?"

"I have to admit, this one has me a little intrigued. But that's hardly a surprise. If out of the blue I'd told you I was a spy you'd feel the same."

"Probably." Reaching out, Mark took her by the hips and pulled her onto his lap. He pressed his face into her hair at her ear and inhaled. "I've always loved the way you smell."

She took his face in her hands and gave him a quick

kiss on the lips. "I want to ask you another question," she said. "It's important to tell me the truth and I won't hold your answer against you, whatever it is. I suppose it doesn't really matter if you had to kill somebody in the line of duty, but I've got to know the truth about the Lindsay girls. Are there many? Have you ever had to seduce some gorgeous enemy agent or anything like that?"

Mark threw back his head and laughed, really laughed. "Arianna, you've seen too many movies."

"I notice you haven't answered my question," she said indignantly.

"I haven't had to seduce any beautiful enemy agents. Or any ugly ones, for that matter. And no, there aren't any Lindsay girls...with one possible exception."

She raised her eyebrows. "If you mean me, I didn't know you were 007, so that doesn't count."

"You can be the first who knows who she's getting then," he said, nuzzling her, letting his warm breath spill over her neck.

A tremor went through her. "Really, the first?"

"Cross my heart."

She pulled back so she could look into his eyes. "I notice you didn't say, 'Hope to die.'"

He grinned. "That's a dangerous thing to say in this line of work."

Before she could think of a retort, there was a knock on the door. They both looked toward it.

"That's either a courier with a secret message," he said, "or it's dinner."

"Oh, Mark," she said, getting to her feet, "you say so

many crazy things, I don't know what to believe and what not to believe."

"Sometimes it's better not to know," he said, giving her a wink. He went to the door and opened it.

A chubby woman was standing there with a tray. "I have two meals for you."

"Wonderful," Mark said. "Come on in."

The woman, who appeared wholesome and home-spun, nodded at Arianna as she carried the tray to the table and put it down. "There are two plates, and coffee," she said. "I hope that'll be all right."

"I'm sure it'll be fine," Mark replied.

The woman left and he went to the table.

Lifting the metal cover from one, he said, "It looks like here we have ham, green beans and whipped potatoes. And here," he said, lifting the other, "we have ham, green beans and whipped potatoes. What sounds good?"

"Actually," she said as she joined him, "I think I'd like the ham, green beans and whipped potatoes."

"Excellent choice, *madame*," he said, and put his arm around her shoulders. "I sense some real compatibility here."

"It's either that or starvation," she said, looking down at the plate. "You know, I'm glad you insisted on ordering dinner, I'm suddenly hungry."

"Must be the missiles on the walls," he said.

Arianna gave him a look. "Come on, James, let's eat and leave your libido for later."

SHE PUSHED her plate back from the table. It had been a pleasant meal, not so much because of the food, which was only passable, but because of the company. It was like the best of times during their engagement but with an added twist, a dollop of something special. The explanation was obvious. Mark was more than she had known and, maybe even more important, more than she was sure she could safely handle.

He had finished his meal and was watching her, leaning back in his chair, his arms folded over his chest. She smiled and he smiled in return.

"Know what?" she said. "You scare me a little."

"You mentioned that before. Do you like it?"

"It's...interesting. I'll spare you the shock of saying it's exciting, though that's probably more accurate."

"Why the admission?"

"I guess I'm trying to understand my feelings. And if I'm misreading the situation, I suppose I'm counting on you to disabuse me of my illusions."

"The very last thing I'd do is disabuse my first Lindsay girl of her illusions."

She smiled, not recalling their ever having conversations quite this playful, yet so candid. Perhaps it had been there, but for whatever reason, she'd missed it. She ran her fingers through her hair, stretching as she did. "What a day. I must look like hell."

"To the contrary, you look beautiful."

"Are superheroes allowed to talk that way? Surely you have a mystique to maintain."

He grinned. "I'm still human." Lowering his voice, he added, "And I still love you, Arianna. I've never been afraid of saying it in the past, and I'm not afraid of saying it now."

His gaze was unwavering. She felt herself blush but she forced herself to look into his eyes.

"What are you thinking?" he asked.

She contemplated him, knowing that the way she answered would set the tone for the rest of the evening, if not for the rest of her stay. But how could she tell him everything that was on her mind? She'd experienced a thousand different moods since she got out of bed that morning...and so many jolts. She'd faced fear and danger and she'd even seen death. Yet there had been good things about this day, as well.

"Having trouble answering?"

Arianna nodded.

He smiled. "Well, sweetpea, actions speaks louder than words."

Mark got up, came around the table and, without the slightest hesitation, pulled her to her feet and kissed her on the mouth.

After the kiss was over, she sighed. "What a difference a day makes."

"Funny, you seem pretty much the same to me."

"Except that my mouth has been hanging open all day."

He brushed her cheek with the back of his fingers. "So, does the notion of being a Lindsay girl intrigue you?"

"I'm almost afraid to answer that."

"Why? Don't you trust me?"

"Twenty-four hours ago I'd have said yes without hesitation...but now..."

He grinned, then kissed the end of her nose. "I can see there's need for a little confidence-building. Why don't you get into something more comfortable so we can discuss this further?"

"What I'd really like to do is take a shower."

"That's within the rules," he said, his eyebrow lilting slightly.

"I suppose there's no point in me saying wait here," she said. "But I'll say it anyway." Turning, she went off to the bathroom.

Once inside the small room, she turned on the water, then took off her sweater and bra. She was unfastening her jeans when the door swung open. She folded her arms over her breasts. Mark stood in the doorway.

"I knew I was wasting my breath," she said. It was false bravado on her part. She'd seen the designs in his eyes and knew this was inevitable.

"We're on my turf, sweetpea," he said.

"And I'm your prisoner?"

"My guest."

"I'm afraid to ask just what that means."

Grinning his delight, Mark stepped over to where she stood, modestly hugging herself. He took her face in his hands and gently kissed her lips. Then he ran his finger over the tops of her breasts. Arianna did not move, but a tremor went through her. He bent and kissed her bare shoulder and her neck. She moaned, letting her head drop back. Her eyes closed. She let her arms fall to her sides. It was his turf, his show and yes, in a very real way, she was his prisoner.

10

WHEN ARIANNA STEPPED into the shower, Mark climbed in right behind her. The water pressure was high, and she felt warm needles of spray on her face and chest as he crossed his arms under her breasts and began caressing her nipples. Then he leaned down to nibble the shell of her ear.

Arianna moaned, wanting to turn into his embrace and kiss him, but he would not let her. Instead, he moved one hand between her legs. The sensuousness of his touch made her tremble, and she gasped.

"Oh, Mark. Don't stop."

Her head sagged back against his chest so that the spray ran over her face. Exquisite sensation came at her from above and below. Arianna closed her eyes, luxuriating in it.

At first he only teased her, his fingertips lightly skimming her, then feathering up across her mound, then down to her inner thigh. But no matter where he touched her, it never seemed to be quite enough. She wanted what he wouldn't give her. Finally, when she didn't think she could take the teasing any longer, Mark slipped one finger into her wet center. Arianna tried to thrust against his hand, to get more of the sweet sensation, but he stayed in control, meting out her pleasure in small enough doses to keep her on the edge.

It was torture, but the sweetest torture she had ever known. Arianna thought she would die of ecstasy. Yet it wasn't enough. She wanted to kiss him, to touch him as he was touching her. But Mark still would not let her move. She was the prisoner of his finger and the spray, the spray and his finger.

Soon she was so overwhelmed by sensation that she couldn't hold back any longer. And when she had finished throbbing, she felt so weak she thought she would collapse. She opened her eyes, turned in his arms and looked at Mark. He was rock-hard. She wanted him again. Right then. She wanted him inside her.

Mark lifted her and she wrapped her legs around his waist. His shaft was at her opening. He slipped into her and filled her so completely that she cried out.

"Oh, Mark. Oh, don't stop."

He began thrusting. She gyrated against him, cries of pleasure coming from her lips as she rode him. Mark backed her against the wall as she clung to him, moaning with each penetration. He was so deep, so hard, that he forced the breath out of her. But Arianna didn't care. For the first time ever, she completely surrendered to him. Mark controlled her pleasure, her body, her very life.

When Mark thrust into her a final time, she came, her orgasm so intense that she would have collapsed if he wasn't holding her. He let her legs slide from his waist, but before they touched the floor he scooped her into his arms and carried her to the bed, where he put her down.

She was sopping wet, but she didn't care. Nothing seemed to matter. In the back of her mind she heard the sound of the water stop. A moment later, Mark returned with two towels. He placed one over her, then began drying himself with the other.

She stared at him, knowing intellectually he was the same man she'd made love to dozens and dozens of times, and yet he was someone very different. When he was dry, he began toweling her. Then he lay down and took her hand.

She gave a sigh of deep contentment, feeling her strength returning. "So, I guess I'm now officially a Lindsay girl."

"Yes," he said, kissing her fingers. "I'd say it's official."

THEIR LOVEMAKING HAD BEEN the inevitable conclusion of what had been an incredible day, she thought a short while later as she lay beside him. And though she felt purged, complete, there was also an emptiness that left her vaguely troubled. Mark, the Mark she thought she knew, had been transformed into a sexy stranger. They had made love. But where was his heart?

He rolled his head toward her and drew her hand to his face, pressing it against his cheek. "You okay, Arianna?"

"Yes," she said with a sigh. "Maybe I'm a little overwhelmed by everything."

Mark pulled her against him. "You've had a lot to contend with today," he said, kissing her temple. "I'm sorry. If there'd been an easier way, I'd have spared you. But the important thing is that you relax and let me worry about things from here on out. The worst is behind us."

She was grateful for his reassuring words. Seldom in her life had she put herself completely in someone else's hands. She had today with Mark.

She pulled back to look into his eyes. But there was not enough ambient light from the open bathroom door to read his expression. "How long have you been a secret agent?"

"About three years. Quite a while before we met."

"Yes. But you're still fairly new at it."

"Too new. It only took three guys at the chalet to subdue me, I'm ashamed to say. Next time I'll be better prepared."

She ran her hand over his chest. To think that from the day they had met he had been living a double life. Mark had said he truly loved her, that being a spy had nothing to do with his feelings. She wondered if that was really true.

"Did you ever feel guilty about keeping me in the dark?" she asked.

"I would have if it had had an impact on our lives, but it didn't."

She sighed. "I never questioned what you were doing whenever you made trips abroad, but once we were married, I might have gotten curious and asked. What would you have done?"

"Protected you from things you didn't need to know."

She propped her head on her hand, looking him

square in the eye. "That would work for things you didn't *want* me to know, too. Like secret escapades with your Lindsay girls."

"There weren't any, Arianna. Honest."

"No secret rendezvous in a Moscow nightclub or furtive lovemaking in a Paris hotel?"

"Nope," he said. "Not even once."

"I would have thought the women would have thrown themselves at you."

"Well, I dated, of course. But you knew that."

"Did any of them know about your double life?" She ran her free hand over his shoulder.

"In this business, discretion is the name of the game," he said with a crooked grin. "All communication is on a need-to-know basis."

She kissed his stubborn chin. "So, even if you were tortured, you wouldn't talk."

"There's torture...and there's torture," he said.

She ran her hand over his hard stomach to his loins. "Is this the sort of torture that might work?"

He laughed. "You'll be the last to know, believe me."

Arianna gave him a big hug, then she lay back down beside him. She suddenly felt exhausted. "If I hadn't seen those troops and the helicopters and those bodies with my own eyes, I would never have believed it," she said.

"Seeing is believing, sweetpea."

Arianna glanced over at his watch lying on the bedside table. She picked it up. "Looks like an ordinary watch," she said.

"The wonders of modern technology."

"And to think, all I had to do was turn this little knob."

"Careful," Mark said. "This is one time we don't need a paramilitary strike force."

He caressed her head and for a while they lay quietly in each other's arms.

"I know there are questions I should ask," she murmured. "I know I should be assuming responsibility for myself, but you know what?"

"What, sweetpea?"

"This is one time that I'm willing to put myself completely in your hands."

"That's exactly the way it should be," he said.

"No, Mark, it's not. I'm just too emotionally spent to object."

"As long as I feel you're safe, you can have it any way you want, Arianna."

He wasn't exactly agreeing, but he *was* expressing his concern for her safety. It was hard to be critical of that, even if it flew in the face of everything she believed. The question, of course, was what tomorrow would bring—or the day after that. Until then, she could only be glad she was Mark's prisoner, and not the prisoner of somebody else.

IT WAS A FEW MINUTES after 6:00 a.m. when Mark awoke. There being no windows, the clock was the only reliable indicator of time. But they had left the bathroom light on with the door slightly ajar, which enabled some light to spill into the room. Arianna was sleeping deeply, but he couldn't resist the temptation to take her sweet little body in his arms. So he hugged her, bringing a mild groan of complaint in response. She soon settled back down, seemingly content.

It had been another magical night—though this one might even have topped what they'd shared in Vail. He sensed a new dimension in her and there was no doubt in his mind it was in response to his own transformation. The irony again struck him—the more he challenged her, the more positively she responded. And yet there was enough of the old Mark in him that he couldn't be indifferent or heartless.

But his triumph also had its downside. What would happen when she discovered that things were not quite as they appeared? An enticing identity was a bit like being wealthy—a man could never be sure he was wanted for himself. In short, he needed to know how she felt about *him*, the man behind the image.

But it was hard to complain. Arianna had given him as much pleasure as he had given her. After they'd recovered from the first time, they'd made love again. The mood had been different. Ari had seemed more like a tiger than a kitten. She'd held nothing back.

In a way, though, it was a hollow victory. They still faced enormous problems. She had been chastened, but how long would that last? Eventually their bedroom spy fantasy wouldn't be enough to keep her occupied. She would turn to the manuscript then and he would be faced with the same old dilemma—how to dissuade her from proceeding with her project until he was sure it was safe?

True, editing the damn thing would keep her busy for a while. He'd already decided to scrounge a computer so she could work, but that wasn't a solution.

How much time he had was hard to say—a few days to a week, perhaps.

Mark decided to get cleaned up. He slipped on his pants and crossed the hall to his own room so as not to awaken Arianna. Just as he closed the door, the phone rang. He picked up the receiver. It was Marcia Allen, his administrative assistant in New York.

"I know it's early," she said, "but I wanted to give you as much notice as possible. I've checked with everybody and the earliest the French and Germans can reschedule is after the first of the year. There's a conflict for someone on every alternative date between now and then. So what do you want to do?"

"Damn," he said. "Wouldn't you know it. This is a very bad time to be leaving."

"Shall I set it for January, then?"

"No," Mark said, rubbing his jaw. "I've got to put that deal together. It's now or never."

"Everything's set up for Monday afternoon here in our office with time blocked out for Tuesday, as well. Do you want me to arrange transportation for you to get back?"

"No, I'll take care of it from here. I have no idea what my schedule will be, but I'll have to spend a couple of hours in the office before the meeting, which means I'll be arriving Monday morning at the latest."

"Okay," Marcia said. "Need anything else?"

"How's Dad's mood been the past few days?"

"Growing impatience. He's been grumbling about your hobby, as he calls it."

"I can't blame him. Does he know where I am at the moment?"

"I haven't said anything to him since I told him you were in Colorado. I'm not sure where you are myself."

"I'm not either, to be honest. But as far as Dad's concerned, let's leave things as they are," Mark said. "No sense creating complications unnecessarily."

"Right."

"Thanks, Marcia."

"Good luck with whatever it is you're doing. I assume it's more of the same."

"Actually not. This is a little different."

"Then I won't ask."

"See you in a couple of days." Mark hung up the phone and groaned. That he couldn't get the meeting pushed back meant he'd have to leave Arianna here alone, and something told him that wasn't a very good idea. But he had no choice.

Mark took off his pants and headed for the bathroom. He always enjoyed a nice hot shower in the morning, but after the one he'd had last night with Arianna, showers would never be the same.

WHEN ARIANNA AWOKE, she thought she was at Mark's place in New York. Then she remembered they were no longer engaged, though she was certain she'd slept with him. Though sleep had nothing to do with it.

Sighing at the memories of the previous night, she rolled over. But Mark was not beside her in the narrow bed. Then it finally all came tumbling back. She was deep underground at spy headquarters and last night she'd had a very good time.

"Oh, Mark," she said aloud, unable to help the smile on her face.

But where was he? She checked the time. It was nearly nine. Lord, she'd really slept in. It was little wonder. What a night!

Mark had been absolutely fabulous. Of course she'd been in a receptive mood, a *very* receptive mood. She writhed on the bed, taking pleasure at the recollection of their lovemaking. On the other hand she had to consider what it meant and where it was leading, though she really didn't want to think about that just yet. She wanted to savor the feeling, if only for a little while.

There was another consideration, however. Breakfast. Damn, if she wasn't hungry. She wondered if Mark was waiting for her so they could eat together. Either way, she had to get a move on because the cafeteria would be closing soon. Maybe she'd find Mark there, if he wasn't in his room.

She quickly showered, did her hair and makeup, and dressed. As she was putting on her earrings, her eyes fell on the phone. She wondered if it was hard to get an outside line should she want to give Jerry a call. She picked up the receiver, but there was no dial tone. The phone was dead. What did that mean? That they didn't trust her? What else?

Ruminating over how she felt about that, she left her room. She found a note taped to her door. It was from Mark and it said he was trying to find her a computer so she could work. That made her feel better. It pleased her that he was so considerate—not that he hadn't always been, but now it was coming from a different person and she liked it. She liked a lot of things about this new Mark.

As she made her way along the corridor, Arianna

pondered the fact that all this excitement was happening with a man who she'd not only known for a long time, but had intended to marry. That had to be significant, but she couldn't say what it meant to her or Mark. All she knew for sure was that she'd have a lot to think about over the coming days.

As she passed through the lobby area on her way to the cafeteria, Arianna noticed workmen coming out of the double doors opposite the elevators. She did not get a good look at what was behind them, but she saw a sign that said Authorized Personnel Only. Her first thought was that must be where all the sneaky stuff went on.

When another workman came out, wedging a door open, Arianna hesitated for a moment. She was just too curious to pass up an opportunity to see what was behind the secret doors. From her vantage point she couldn't see much, so she casually ambled to the door. As she neared, three or four workmen came out and, judging by the thermoses and lunch pails, they were going on a break.

Once they'd disappeared down the corridor, Arianna stepped inside the restricted area. The space was a sort of anteroom enclosed in glass. Beyond the glass walls was an even larger space with high ceilings. The dominant feature on the big wall opposite her was a gigantic map of the northern hemisphere from the perspective directly above the North Pole. At the center bottom of the map was the United States. A large red dot marked a spot in the middle of northern Montana. Arianna assumed that was where they were.

The room was in disarray, as though it was in the

process of being disassembled. A large flat table was in the middle of the room. Several cardboard boxes were stacked on top of it, as well as various tools. Wires and cables protruded from the walls in many places and it appeared that whatever had been there had been ripped out. Off to the sides were smaller rooms behind glass walls, which overlooked the main room.

It appeared to her that the place had once been some sort of command center, a military facility in all probability. Deciding there was no more to see, she went back out to the lobby. To her relief, there was nobody around. Not certain what to make of what she'd seen, Arianna proceeded to the cafeteria. There was nothing extraordinary about it, the usual stainless-steel fixtures, a couple of dozen tables and molded plastic chairs spread over a linoleum floor. The walls were pale, pale yellow trimmed in gray and decorated with lithographs of military aircraft and missiles. A pattern was developing, Arianna decided.

There was hardly anyone in the room, which was not surprising since she had arrived at the very end of the service. Two men who looked to be Japanese and were wearing white shirts and tan pants were huddled over cups of tea in the middle of the room. An older man and a young woman were seated in the corner. A single cafeteria worker stood behind the serving counter.

Arianna went to the end where the trays were located and took some flatware and a napkin. She slid her tray along the counter, taking a bowl of fruit. She was about to take a muffin when a woman came sliding a tray along behind her. The woman was tall, pleasant-looking and had a sweet smile.

"Looks like the early birds got all the worms," she said, indicating the sparse offerings.

"Yes, it does," Arianna replied.

The woman didn't say anything more, but it was nice to hear a sign of friendliness. She proceeded to where the server waited, a young man who looked very much as though he wanted to go home. There wasn't much hot food left. Some scrambled eggs had been scraped into a corner of one of the serving pans. In another there were a dozen strips of bacon and some sausage.

"That appears to be my choice," she said to the young man.

"Unless you want some Japanese breakfast soup and rice," he replied lethargically.

"No, just some eggs, please."

The man spooned eggs onto a plate and handed it to her. Arianna proceeded along, helping herself to orange juice and coffee. She carried her tray to a table next to the one vacated by the two Japanese men who'd left since her arrival. As she unloaded her tray, the woman who'd been behind her in line approached.

"Would you mind company?" she asked. A pained expression filled her face. "I hate eating alone, especially when I'm underground."

"No, I don't mind," Arianna said. "Please."

As the woman unloaded her tray, Arianna recalled Mr. Jones's warning about avoiding the staff. But she hadn't made the overture and she could hardly be expected to be impolite.

"My name's Kate Throop," the dark-haired woman said, pushing her glasses up off her nose. She was in her late forties, affable, rosy-cheeked, engaging.

"Arianna Hamilton."

"Have you been with Consolidated long?"

"Pardon me?"

"With the company."

Arianna assumed it was a euphemism, insider jargon. "Oh, no. I'm actually a sort of visitor."

"Really? Odd place to visit."

"Well, they're odd circumstances."

"I've only been here a week myself," Kate said, sipping her coffee. "Another week and I'll be gone, thank goodness."

Arianna knew she wasn't supposed to ask questions, but Kate Throop was the one who'd taken the initiative and it didn't sound as if she was all that much of an insider. It hardly seemed like the end of the world to engage in a little conversation.

"Have you been with the *company* long?" she asked after taking a long drink of orange juice.

"Oh, I'm not employed by Consolidated," Kate said. "I'm an outside consultant. Personnel's my specialty. As you might imagine, they have real trouble getting people to work here. I was hired to prepare a study on what they can do to make employment more appealing." She lowered her voice. "I hate to say it, but moving to civilization is the best thing they could do, but of course they don't want to hear that."

"Why? For security reasons?"

"No, because they got such a good deal on the site. The government practically gave it to them."

Arianna was confused. "The government?"

"Yes. The government didn't need it anymore. Not with the end of the Cold War."

Arianna blinked.

"This is a former nuclear missile base. Didn't you know that?"

"No, I didn't."

"The Japanese don't seem to mind coming here," Kate said, cutting a piece off her pastry, "but they're mostly technical people. It's not economical to bring them in to serve food, do the maintenance and custodial work, that sort of thing. With the nearest town forty miles away, it's not easy to lure people here, believe me." She popped a bite of pastry into her mouth.

Arianna was really confused now. She could only assume that Kate Throop was not aware of the secret mission that at least some of the people here were engaged in. "What does Consolidated do, exactly?" she asked innocently.

Kate seemed as surprised as Arianna. "Research on satellite communications. It's a joint venture between an American and a Japanese firm. Weren't you aware?"

Arianna shrugged. "I had a general idea."

"I'm doing my best, and I've come up with some proposals, but short of building a new city out here, all they can do that'll ensure a labor supply is provide more amenities and offer terrific pay scales. But that's no surprise. Money's too often the bottom line."

Arianna ate as she listened to Kate talk. The fact that the woman's work had nothing to do with what Mark was involved in gave her pause. Did that mean that his work was so secret it was hidden inside an elaborate front organization that even the outside consultants weren't aware of?

"Personally, I'm eager to get back to California," Kate was saying. "I took this assignment because Terry, he's my husband, was on a temporary assignment here in Montana and I came with him. He travels all over the world."

"Is he with the company?"

"No, no. He's with another high-tech firm."

The thought crossed Arianna's mind that she was being tested, but then she decided that was paranoid. Kate Throop would have to be either the world's best actress or as innocent as she. They were probably both in the dark about what was really going on here.

"You know what I miss most?" Kate said, beaming. "My granddaughter, Emma. Emma Rose Held is her full name and she's just a delight."

"How old is she?"

"Two and a half."

"That's a great age," Arianna said, though her knowledge of children was limited.

As Kate talked about her granddaughter, Arianna thought about a conversation she'd had with Mark about children shortly after they'd become engaged. "I don't want to rush into anything," he'd said, "but for the record, I've always kind of liked kids. When the time's right, a couple of rug rats would be nice."

For Arianna, "when the time's right" had been the operative words. She'd never had a strong urge to be a mother. But then, she hadn't felt much of an urge to be a wife, either.

Sitting three hundred and fifty feet underground, listening to Kate Throop talk about little Emma Rose, the question hit her—did she feel differently about Mark now? If he slipped that ring back on her finger, would she want to pull it off, or would she feel a surge of joy? It occurred to her the answer depended on which Mark they were talking about.

And how did he feel about it? The new Mark Lindsay had said he loved her, but he hadn't said a word about his ring, marriage, children or any of the rest. The most she could say about any understanding between them was that once they were home and life was back to normal, they might give it another try. But even that was vague.

"Arianna?"

She blinked, realizing Kate had asked her a question. "I'm sorry," she said. "I'm afraid I've been preoccupied lately."

"I've been going on and on, I realize."

"No, no, it's me," Arianna said. "I've had a rough couple of days. What did you ask?"

"Just what do you do?"

"Oh." Arianna realized there were a number of ways to answer. She could say she met with celebrities to talk about the literary potential of their lives, that she played cat-and-mouse games with the Mafia, or that she engaged in sexual liaisons with secret agents. But she opted for the safest and most prosaic. "I edit books, Kate," she said. "In New York."

"Then what are you doing here?"

Arianna was considering alternative ways to answer

when she saw Mark coming through the door. "To have an affair with a spy," she said.

Kate laughed. "In other words, it's none of my business."

"No, I wasn't being flip. I just can't tell you the truth. It's classified."

Kate gave her a knowing look as Mark came up to the table.

"Good morning," he said. "Got your breakfast, I see."

Arianna introduced him to Kate. "I was hearing all about Emma Rose," she explained to Mark. "Kate's two-and-a-half-year-old granddaughter in California loves makeup, especially nail polish, animals, bugs, gardening and all kinds of *make-believe*."

"Hey," he said, "my kind of kid."

"Yeah," Arianna said. "I thought so, too."

There was a startled look on his face. Arianna smiled. How nice that for once she'd been able to surprise him!

11

NICE THAT you've made a friend," Mark said as they walked toward their rooms.

"Don't worry, Kate's an outside consultant. In fact, I'm not sure whether or not she knows what really goes on here."

"Either way, it's probably best not to discuss it with her," he said.

"I didn't discuss what you do, Mark, not that I know. After all, I have no desire to get lined up against a wall and shot."

"I don't think the punishment would be quite that severe," he said with a laugh.

They walked through the lobby. She glanced at the door accessing the restricted area. "Are you ever going to tell me what it is you actually do?" she asked.

"Is your curiosity getting the best of you?"

"Well, some things I've figured out for myself. Like this was once a nuclear missile base."

"The underground facilities are a giveaway, I suppose."

"Yes, but some things don't add up," she said as they entered the corridor leading to their rooms. "For example, it's clear that not everyone here is a spy. Some legitimate work is being done in this place."

"Maybe we need to have a talk," he said, not exactly sounding pleased.

Arianna didn't want to make him angry, but it seemed only fair that he show a certain amount of candor. But Mark didn't say anything more until they came to his room.

"I managed to scrounge a computer, and I had it loaded with WordPerfect," he said as he unlocked his door. "Now you ought to be able to work."

He stepped aside so she could enter. She went in, immediately noticing the computer on the table.

As she went over to it, Mark sat down on the bed, giving her an appraising look. But he still hadn't told her what he wanted to talk about.

"Well," she said. "I'm ready. You did say it was time for us to talk?" She sat down in the chair next to the bed.

"We took this site over from the military because of the security it affords and the communications facilities that were available."

"Who's we? Consolidated?"

He blinked. "How do you know about Consolidated?"

"Kate. But I didn't ask her. She volunteered the information. And she was the one who brought it up, not me."

Mark seemed uncomfortable. "Consolidated is a front," he said.

"That's what I figured. A front for the CIA."

"No, the CIA's not involved. I work for a special intelligence organization called Alpha. Our mission is essentially to conduct commercial espionage."

"*Commercial* espionage?"

"The real battle among the nations of the world is being fought on the commercial plane. While the United States promotes free enterprise, it's in the government's interest to ensure that the heavy flow of international commerce and the activities of transnational companies does not become hostile to the legitimate security interests of the country. In effect, we're the security force of the twenty-first century."

"What you're saying is you're a banker spy."

"In a manner of speaking."

She crossed her legs. "So there aren't poison capsules and secret assassinations of enemy agents and all that James Bond stuff."

"No, the only thing I have in common with 007 is the Lindsay girls," he said with a wink.

"But I'm the first, right?"

"Right."

"I don't know why I should believe that," she intoned, recrossing her legs. "You managed to deceive me about who you are during our entire engagement."

His eyes drifted down her, seemingly shifting from the role of spy to lover. "Arianna, it wasn't a matter of being someone other than the man you knew. I'm simply *more* than what you knew."

"But what if you'd found out I was secretly moonlighting as a hooker or something? Wouldn't it make you uneasy?"

He frowned. "I think the two are a little different."

"So you say."

"The important thing," Mark said, "is you're safe,

you have your manuscript to work on and you know my secrets."

What he said was true and she knew she should be satisfied with that, but she wasn't. She couldn't exactly say why—unless it was that she felt out of control. Mark, the Mafia, Alpha, the government, everybody had their hands on the controls in one way or another. Everyone but her.

"I'm afraid I have one unfortunate piece of news," he said. "I'm going to have to leave for a few days."

"On a secret mission?"

He smiled. "Let's just say on business."

"And of course I have to stay here."

"Don't you agree it would be best? I mean, look what's happened."

"Yes, Mark, but I can't hide out in a nuclear missile silo for the rest of my life."

He got up and went over to the chair where she sat and touched her cheek. "I don't like this any more than you do, Arianna. As you recall, it was forced on us."

"Yes," she lamented. "But I feel so helpless."

"Look," he said, taking her hand and pulling her to her feet. "I promise we'll sort things out so you can go back to New York."

"How do you propose to do that?" she asked as he gathered her into his arms.

Mark stroked her hair. "I'll work on that while I'm gone. I haven't figured it out in detail, but I've got some ideas."

"Which your oath of secrecy prevents you from sharing."

He lifted her chin, smiling into her eyes. "I know it's asking a lot," he said, "but can you trust me this once?"

It was an unusual request, but these were unusual circumstances. And she owed Mark and his friends in Alpha a great deal. "All right," she said. "I'll trust you. With one qualification."

"What's that?"

"I'm not making an open-ended commitment. I want to know that within a reasonable period of time—a matter of days—I'll be free to go on with my life."

"That's fair."

Arianna felt better. The solution wasn't ideal, but they'd both been constructive and, best of all, Mark seemed sensitive to her needs. She thought of how he hadn't changed in that respect.

"What's going on in that pretty head of yours?" he asked, brushing her cheek with his knuckles.

"I've surrendered my body, Agent Lindsay, I'm not going to turn my thoughts over to you. Even Lindsay girls are entitled to their secrets."

He kissed her lightly on the lips and smiled.

"So, when do you leave?" she asked.

"Tomorrow."

"Then this is our last day together."

"For a while, anyway. Three or four days at most."

Arianna peered into his eyes, not nearly so certain what was lurking there as she'd once been. "I probably shouldn't admit it, but I'm starting to miss you already."

"I know I'll miss you," he said.

Again she thought about the future, what it would

be like when all this was over. She felt certain they'd be seeing each other, but things would be different now. That was all to the good, of course. But there was also uncertainty.

"The question," Mark said, "is how you want to spend your day."

"I get to choose?"

"Yes."

"What are my choices?"

"If your work is calling, I'll get out of your hair," he said. "On the other hand, I can take you for a drive in the country. Or we can hang out here. Whatever feels good to you, Arianna."

She considered that. "Well, if I'm going to be holed up here for a few days, there'll be plenty of time to work and get cabin fever in the process. I guess I'll opt for the fresh air."

"Great! I'll get a jeep. There's a recreation area at a small lake in the mountains. It's for the use of the staff. We can go there, maybe have a picnic lunch."

"I'd enjoy that, Mark."

"Meanwhile, why don't I take the computer to your room. I also got a scanner so you can put the manuscript on the hard drive. That is how you prefer to work, isn't it?"

"Yes. That'll be terrific."

Mark picked up the computer and monitor. Arianna went to the door and opened it before stepping across the hall to unlock her door. As Mark plugged in the equipment, she went back to his room for the scanner. It was then that she noticed his phone. On an impulse she stepped over and picked up the receiver. There was a dial tone. Apparently, visitors were the only ones who weren't trusted.

ARIANNA HAD NEVER BEEN much of a nature buff, but the crisp Montana air and bright sunshine was proving to be an elixir. They were in the jeep Mark had borrowed, driving along a gravel road toward the mountains. She felt giddy as she reveled in the freedom.

The road started winding into the foothills. The prairie grasses and shrubs gave way to scrub pine, with deep forests visible on the slopes ahead. Arianna glanced over at Mark, still marveling at the mystery of him. It was clear that he'd pulled strings to bring her to this place. And for Alpha to have assumed a risk with no particular benefit, Mark had to be valuable to them. But how valuable?

What did he do that allowed him to live a double life without being detected, even by the woman he'd intended to marry? Or was it that she'd been so self-centered, so involved with her own life, that she'd never noticed what was right in front of her nose?

"You know, Mark," she said, "now that there's been time for it to sink in, I have to tell you I'm kind of embarrassed that you've been living this whole other life and I didn't have a clue."

"I wouldn't have been much of an operative if it had been obvious."

"Still..."

"So, how do you feel about my little hobby now that you've had a day to think about it?"

She thought for a moment or two. "I guess I think it's kind of neat. I hate to gush, but it's true."

Mark smiled.

"Don't let it go to your head, though," she warned.

He studied the road before them, the wind blowing his brown hair. Mark frequently wore sunglasses, as now, but at the moment he struck her as particularly mysterious and elusive. Why hadn't she been able to see it before?

"Does it bother you that the cat's out of the bag?" she asked. "I mean, every time you leave town for a few days I'll know. Or wonder."

"Do you plan on keeping track of me?"

Arianna realized she'd assumed a fact not in evidence, as Zara liked to say. Their future, if there was to be one, remained an open question.

"Dealing with a spy is trickier than I imagined," she said. "I bet nothing ever got past you."

"Shall I tell you what Richard Gere ordered the night you had dinner with him?"

Her mouth sagged open. "Mark, you didn't!"

He chuckled. "No, I don't abuse the resources at my disposal."

"Unless it's saving a former fiancée from the Mafia."

"I will make exceptions," he said.

Feeling brazen, Arianna reached over and gave his knee a squeeze. Mark smiled. There was no disputing it—the chemistry between them was different. And she liked it.

As they climbed higher into the mountains, the scent of pine grew stronger. She was so absorbed in this new Mark that she wouldn't have traded anything to be back in New York just then—though she was still looking forward to taking her manuscript to the Big Apple and getting it published. But she was also curious about what would happen between her and Mark. A few months ago their relationship was a source of anxiety. Now it was pure excitement.

Finally they came to the lake and the two modest little cabins on its shore. Mark parked near one of the cabins. There was no one else around. They decided to take a walk before lunch, maybe hike around the lake.

Mark put their lunch in the cabin so it would be safe from animals, then came down the steps to where she waited. He extended his hand and she slipped her fingers into his large palm. Although this was more the sort of outing her sister would enjoy, Arianna felt happy. Mark was no stranger, but this had all the characteristics of new love. Maybe she'd end up yet with the man she'd refused to marry.

THE WIND WAS MOANING and Arianna pulled the blanket up under her chin and thought again about the bear they'd seen at the edge of the woods just before sunset. She knew that with winter approaching, the critters had a ravenous appetite, but Mark had assured her that little strawberry blondes were not a part of their diet. "When did you become an expert on wildlife?" she'd asked him. "Is it part of the training?" He'd laughed. "Yeah. You never know when you might be called on to parachute into Siberia with a suitcase full of foreign currency," he'd quipped.

That had been a couple of hours earlier. Rather than rush back to the compound, they'd built a fire in one of the cabins. Their picnic lunch, provided by the cafeteria, had been uninspired, but in the crisp autumn air, it tasted good—almost as good as one of the many gourmet lunches in New York she'd been forced, under pressure of time, to gulp down before hurrying back to work.

Mark had pulled the mattress off the bed and put it in front of the rustic stone fireplace. Not unexpectedly, they'd ended up making love.

"This was the way it was supposed to be in Vail," Mark said as he stared into the fire.

Arianna ran her hand over his bare chest, liking the furry texture. Turning her face, she kissed his shoulder. "At least here we won't have to worry about the Mafia barging in," she said. "A bear maybe, but not the Mafia."

"There are always trade-offs," he said.

"Is that an Alpha slogan or the stoic side of Mark Lindsay?"

"Am I sounding stoic?"

"Uh-huh."

"Maybe it's because I'm not too keen on leaving you."

"I'm not too thrilled about it myself," she said.

"Nice to know we're thinking along the same lines."

She drew her fingers through the soft mat of hair on his chest. "Mark, I don't want to be precipitous, and I know you have plenty of reason to refuse, but I want you to know I'd like to have a relationship with you once we're home and everything's back to normal."

"What do you mean by normal?" he asked.

"Actually, that's a good question. Things between us have changed forever."

"Yes, but I'd like to think for the better."

"I would, too," she said, turning her face to him.

Mark kissed her softly. "No pressure," he said. "We'll have to see how things go and take it from there."

Arianna decided she liked that. Despite the cloud hanging over her head, their prospects for the future looked good. It was just a matter of getting from here to there, she figured. From here to there...

12

THEY RETURNED to the compound late. Arianna noticed one curious thing as they entered the gate. The sign at the entrance was no longer covered by a canvas tarp. The sign said Consolidated Industries. She couldn't help wondering if it had been covered the night of their arrival for her benefit and, if so, why, unless because of a general penchant for secrecy. She said nothing to Mark, knowing that in just a matter of hours he'd be leaving. More questions would hardly be conducive to a favorable mood and she wanted last impressions to be good ones.

Arianna read for a while before they went to bed. Mark occupied himself with paperwork that she assumed related to his mission. When they finally slipped under the covers of the narrow bed, they held each other, falling asleep fairly quickly. But as she was drifting off, she had a very strong sense of wanting their relationship back. She told Mark that, whispering her feelings in the darkness. But he was so drowsy, she wasn't at all sure he'd heard.

Arianna herself fell into a deep sleep and was only half-aware of him kissing her around four or five in the morning, before crawling from the bed and going off on his trip. She awoke to a painful sense of his absence.

Arianna had an early breakfast. She sat at a table

alone and didn't attempt to speak with anyone. However, she did listen to some of the conversations around her. The ones in Japanese she couldn't understand, but the ones in English weren't terribly revealing, either. There certainly wasn't any spy talk. What work-related conversations she did hear seemed to pertain to satellites and communications devices. That made her wonder how many of these people worked for Alpha and how many for Consolidated.

After breakfast she went to her room to work. The scanner had been a good idea. She went through the manuscript page by page, putting it on the hard disk. It was a long and tedious process, but an excellent way to have a backup copy.

The task completed, she began working on the book itself. It would end up being a virtual rewrite. Sal Corsi was no literary genius, but he did have a knack for assembling materials. She had everything she needed to whip the book into shape.

She got so immersed in her work that by the time she began feeling hunger pangs again and checked her watch, she'd very nearly missed the lunch hour. The food would be on a par with the picnic lunch she and Mark had eaten the day before, but the ambience and the company couldn't possibly compare.

Arianna arrived in the cafeteria with only five minutes to spare. To her surprise and pleasure, Kate Throop was just going through the line.

"Oh, hi," she said, seeing Arianna. "Want me to save you a place?"

"That would be great, thanks."

Mark hadn't wanted her to fraternize with staff, but

she already knew Kate and, as she'd rationalized earlier, it couldn't hurt if they talked because Kate was an outsider. Arianna went through the line, taking some whitefish, boiled potatoes and mixed vegetables. Kate was beaming when she got to the table. Arianna was glad for the company.

"You look to be in good spirits," she said to the woman.

"Well, yesterday was a red-letter day."

"Oh?"

"Terry and I got a home video in the mail of Emma Rose."

"Your granddaughter."

"Yes. It was the cutest thing. Of course, I'm completely objective."

Arianna smiled as she took her plate off the tray, which she set on an empty chair. "Let me guess. In the tub with a rubber ducky."

"That was last spring," Kate joked. "No, we have a video of her getting her nails done. She just loves makeup. You ought to see the big smile into the camera as she held up her wet nails for Grandma and Grandpa to see."

"I bet it was adorable," Arianna said.

"Be thankful I don't have a VCR with me." Kate took a bite of her lunch. "So, have you been keeping busy?"

"Yesterday we went up to the lake and had a picnic."

"At the recreation site."

Arianna smiled to herself, thinking of the form of recreation she and Mark had selected. "Yes."

"I checked it out for my evaluation," Kate said.

"Beautiful place, but for the locals it's nothing special, of course. I understand the Japanese and Americans from other parts of the country enjoy it. Fishermen seem to like it a lot."

There was loud laughter from the group of men at the table behind Arianna. Kate glanced at them, amused. She seemed like such a nice woman. Arianna wondered if she was truly oblivious to the presence of Alpha. It was hard to believe that Kate was involved with personnel and yet didn't know that some of the people she was studying were secret agents. Or was it that Kate had been planted there to keep an eye on her?

Over the din of the cafeteria, Arianna heard a man's voice coming from a table behind her. It sounded familiar. Listening, she realized he had an East Coast accent—New York or New Jersey. Did it remind her of someone back home?

Then it struck her. He sounded exactly like the Mafia leader who'd barged into the chalet. How eerie. That guy was dead. Arianna turned to look at him. Of course, the gangsters had been masked, so she didn't know what their features were like, but this guy was of the same general size and body type as the man who'd terrorized them.

Then she saw it! Her eyes rounded. Her fork slipped from her fingers, falling to the floor. The man had a Marine Corps tattoo on the back of his hand—just like the one on the hand of the Mob boss.

He had turned at the sound of the falling fork and glanced into her eyes. He, too, looked momentarily shocked. But then, recovering, he turned back to his companions. His reaction was all the confirmation she needed. It was the same guy!

Arianna's heart began racing. The gangsters had been killed! At least that's what Jones had said. Even if that Mafia leader had managed to escape, why would he be at a secret government installation hundreds of miles from where that gunfight had occurred?

"Are you all right, Arianna?" Kate said, clearly seeing that something was wrong.

Arianna was so tense that she could hardly speak. Taking a quick peek over her shoulder, she was dismayed to see the man leaving his half-eaten lunch on the table. As he neared the door and glanced back at her, there was absolutely no doubt in her mind that this was the man who'd kidnapped her.

"Arianna?"

"Kate, do you see that man leaving?" she said, lowering her voice. "The one at the door in the white shirt and brown pants?"

"Yes."

"Do you know who he is?"

"Well, I believe he's the warehouse supervisor," Kate said, pushing her glasses up off her nose. "Lipski, I think his name is. He's a New Yorker."

"Oh my God," Arianna said, pressing her hands to her mouth. She had no idea what was going on, but she realized with sudden and total clarity that she'd been the object of some sort of grand hoax.

"Are you ill?" Kate asked, looking worried.

The face on the woman across from her was completely innocent, but Arianna was so confused and distraught that she was unable to trust anyone.

"Is there something I can do?" Kate asked, her evident concern growing.

Arianna swallowed hard. Searching the woman's eyes, she decided she needed to confide in someone. Surely the grandmother of a little child named Emma Rose couldn't be complicit with a band of charlatans or spies or gangsters or whatever they were.

"Kate," she said, her voice shaking, "don't answer this if you don't want to. In fact, I'd prefer you say nothing at all rather than lie. But I'd like to know something and please, please tell me the truth. Is this installation the headquarters for a secret government organization called Alpha?"

Kate Throop blinked. "Arianna," she said, her voice gentle, "they have a very good doctor here. I can't vouch for him personally, but I'm familiar with his personnel file. Perhaps you'd like to—"

"I'm not sick or emotionally disturbed," Arianna insisted. "I know that I sound crazy. But I'm certain the man who just left was involved in a scheme to kidnap me by posing as a gangster."

Kate reached across the table, her expression pained as she patted Arianna's hand. "Perhaps if you gave me the name of your...sponsor...whoever brought you here, I could contact him and—"

"Mark's gone. He left this morning on a miss...well, let's say on a business trip. I have no idea if he's aware of what's going on, but I do know one thing for sure, I have to get out of here."

Kate frowned. Arianna knew the poor woman probably thought she was dealing with a delusional paranoid. Well, at the moment Arianna felt paranoid, but with good reason. She was not mistaken. That man was shocked when he'd seen her face. And it was no accident that he'd gotten up and run out like that.

"Look," she said to Kate. "I know what you're thinking. In your shoes I'd think I was nuts, too. But I can prove it to you, if you'll come with me to my room."

Kate Throop glanced around as though she was looking for someone to appeal to for help. "There are other people who're bothered by the isolation," she said in a kindly way. "Normally it takes months rather than days, but—"

"Okay," Arianna said. "I'll make you a deal. Come see the manuscript I have in my room. Read just a bit of it. And if after five minutes you don't believe me, I'll go with you to see the doctor."

"I guess that's fair enough," Kate said. "Do you want to finish lunch first?"

"Frankly, I don't think I could eat. This is going to sound weird, but the guy who just left is supposed to be dead."

KATE SAT ON THE BED, leafing through the first few pages of the manuscript. She was in awe. "I read about that gangster being killed at the airport in New York. And this is his book?"

Arianna pointed to the byline on the title page. "The Mafia killed him, trying to get their hands on this," she explained. "There's a bunch of dirty judges and cops who'll go down if this exposé comes to light, so the Mob is doing everything in its power to prevent that from happening."

"And you think the supervisor in the warehouse here is a gangster?"

"I don't know about that. But I am certain he posed as one in what's beginning to look like a fake kidnapping."

Kate shook her head. "I'm afraid I don't understand. I live a nice quiet life. I've never encountered anything like this before."

Arianna told her about the masked Mafia men who had burst in on her and Mark in Vail, and how Mark, using his connections with Alpha, arranged to have them rescued. "Jones, the leader of the operation, brought us here. I was told this is a secret Alpha facility, and when I asked Mark about Consolidated, he said it was a cover."

"Maybe it's your friend Mark who's a little off," Kate said sympathetically. "I don't know every person who works here, but I've interviewed a large number and I've studied virtually every personnel file to one degree or another, with the exception of the Japanese workers, and I can assure you there's nobody here doing espionage."

"Maybe the Alpha operatives at this particular facility are all Japanese."

"I can't say they aren't, because I haven't worked with them much. But I do know Isao Hayashi, the Japanese personnel officer, quite well. He assured me these people are all highly qualified scientists, engineers and technicians. And observing the long hours they work, I don't know when they'd have time to do any spying."

"The personnel officer could be part of Alpha, too."

"Based on what I know about this place and the people who work here," Kate said, "somebody's been pulling your leg."

"What about the paramilitary troops who rescued us? The helicopters and the executive plane that brought us here?"

"I don't know about troops and helicopters, but I do know Consolidated has a plane for the use of its executives and other VIPs."

Arianna thought. Could this all have been a hoax? If it was, then Mark had to be a part of it. But why? Then it occurred to her. She had been determined to get back to New York as fast as she could, and Mark hadn't wanted her to. Would he have gone to all the trouble of setting this up, just so she wouldn't leave? It had to be! There was no other explanation.

"Kate," she said, turning to her friend, "I've got to get to New York as fast as I can. How do I do it?"

"I guess the quickest would be to go to Great Falls and get a flight out of there, but it's ninety miles away."

"Is there a way I can get there quickly?"

"There's a bus that Consolidated operates for the workers who live here at the facility, but it won't be leaving until tonight."

"I'm not sure they'd let me waltz out of here that easily."

"They?"

"This may not be an Alpha base, but someone is working with Mark to keep me here under false pretenses. That fake Mafia leader with the tattoo is one, and there must be others. I don't know if they'd go so far as to keep me here against my will, but I'd rather not find out the hard way."

"You're saying you want to sneak away."

"Yes. The sooner the better."

Kate thought for a moment. "I've got a car. I was planning on picking up Terry in Great Falls this evening. Since I work on my own time, I can leave whenever I want. I suppose I could drive you."

"Would you mind? I'd be eternally grateful."

"I still can't believe anybody here would be involved in a kidnapping hoax."

"I wouldn't have, either, until now," Arianna said wistfully. "But it's beginning to appear that my former fiancé is more industrious than I thought. To put it mildly, I've been duped."

"When do you want to leave?"

Arianna glanced at her watch. "As soon as I can pack my bags and copy the files from that computer onto a disk."

13

MARK STOOD at the window, looking out at the New York skyline. It was a drizzly Sunday morning, the kind where people tended to stay inside, reading the paper in bed or having a leisurely breakfast in anticipation of an afternoon of football on TV. He had been light-years from that sort of normalcy for days now, and it would be a few more at least before he could relax.

The Federal Building was an unlikely place to be at this hour on a Sunday, but after their meeting last night the FBI had considered the matter sufficiently urgent to bring in the chief of the organized-crime division from Washington and to drag Bud Aronson, the U.S. Attorney for New York, out of bed for an early meeting. They'd been huddled in the next room, conferring, while Mark waited. He'd agonized before making his decision, finally coming to the conclusion that the only way to end this was to bring in the Feds. And so, as soon as he'd arrived in New York, he'd contacted them.

The door opened behind him and two of the men he'd been talking to entered. Walter Evans, head of the organized-crime division, and Hap Murphy, the agent in charge of the New York office. Both wore somber, three-button suits. Evans, a balding man of fifty, had on a white shirt but no tie. Murphy was dark and slight. Both wore grim expressions.

"Bud Aronson had another commitment, so he asked us to finish up," Evans said, gesturing for Mark to join them at the small conference table. Once they were seated, Mark on one side of the table, the two FBI officials on the other, Evans spoke again. "We don't have to tell you the repercussions this is going to have."

"My principal concern is for Arianna."

"It's too bad you didn't bring the manuscript with you," Murphy said.

"Well, I think that's for Arianna to decide. I'm just the intermediary, and I certainly wasn't going to steal it from her. If I can offer her an arrangement she can live with, she's more likely to turn over the manuscript to you."

"That's the problem," Evans said grimly. "She has possession of evidence of numerous crimes which would be used first to indict, and ultimately try, the perpetrators. Bud Aronson is prepared to request the warrants as soon as we have the evidence in our hands."

"But I'm sure Arianna will want assurances that she can use the material for the publication she has planned."

"We can't guarantee that—at least not until the judicial process has run its course."

"There must be some way," Mark argued.

"Look," Murphy said. "You admit that her life's in danger, and possibly yours, as well, so long as she has the evidence. The obvious thing for her to do is turn everything over to us. That way, everybody's safe. Bud says he won't even need her testimony. She'll be out of this. Seems to me it's a no-brainer."

"You don't know Arianna," Mark said glumly.

"The woman obviously has courage," Evans said, "but I'm not so sure about her judgment. My advice is to tell her she has no alternative but to cooperate with us—if she wants to be safe. If she doesn't, she's going to be out there on her own. Considering what she's up against, that's not a very happy prospect."

"Granted," Mark said. "But I can't force her. As it is, I may have earned her eternal enmity."

"Our hands are tied then," Evans said. "The judicial process takes precedence."

"All right," Mark said, realizing he wasn't getting anywhere. "I'll see what I can do to convince her, but don't hold your breath. And now, unless you have any more questions, I think I'll be going."

"What are your plans, Mr. Lindsay?"

"I've got business to tend to starting tomorrow, so I'll be in town for a while."

"I suggest you be very careful. If the Mob knows you've had possession of the manuscript, as it appears they do, they'll likely be looking for you, as well."

"I haven't gone near my apartment, believe me."

"Are you staying in a hotel?"

"No, at a town house I bought a few months back. Ironically, it was where Arianna and I were going to live after our marriage. We were in the process of renovating it when the wedding was called off. This is the first it's been used. I haven't managed to bring myself to move in."

"Sounds like you've been through the wringer with Miss Hamilton," Evans said.

"She's a challenge. A guy's got to have a little ingenuity if he hopes to keep up with her, believe me."

"Based on what I've seen so far," Evans said, "I don't doubt it for a minute."

Mark left the Federal Building, uncertain what, if anything, he'd accomplished. The Feds were into the thing now and maybe somehow, in the long run, that would prove beneficial. But he still hadn't solved his problem with Arianna. He could only keep her holed up at Consolidated's Montana facility so long. Then it would probably come down to a battle of wills.

Mark flagged a taxi and went back to his town house in Gramercy Park. He let himself in. The place was essentially unfurnished, but he'd bought a futon and some linens the previous afternoon, which meant he could sleep and shower in relative comfort. He'd had a phone installed for the use of the workmen who'd done the renovation and had never bothered to disconnect it. That turned out to be fortunate.

As he paced across the hardwood floors of the empty house, Mark began to wonder if he should give Arianna a call. She might be getting cabin fever, even though she had plenty of work to keep her busy. Besides, he wanted to hear her voice and tell her he missed her. Going to the phone, he dialed the number of the main switchboard at Consolidated in Montana.

"Oh, Mr. Lindsay," the operator said. "Mr. Almquist has been trying to reach you. Let me put you through to him."

Mark had a sinking feeling while he waited. Something must have happened to Arianna. It could be anything, but whatever it was, he had a premonition it wasn't good.

Finally, George Almquist, the plant manager, came on the line. "I'm glad you called, Mark," he said. "We've got a problem. Miss Hamilton has left the facility."

"What?"

"I believe she figured out this wasn't a secret installation. I understand she spotted one of the men we sent to Colorado at Jones's request. In any case, she's gone."

Mark groaned. "Well, I suppose it was too much to expect we could fool her for long."

"There was nothing I could do to keep her from leaving," Almquist said. "As you know, we couldn't physically restrain her. My agreement with Jones was that we'd play the game, but I would have to draw the line at force."

"Yeah, yeah, I understand," Mark said. "What I'm concerned about now is Arianna. Do you know where she went?"

"No. Just that she left the facility with Mrs. Throop, one of our outside consultants. I could try to reach Kate and see if she'll tell me where she took Miss Hamilton, if that would help."

"If you don't mind," Mark said. "But I think I have a pretty good idea where she's ultimately headed. When did she leave, exactly?"

"Yesterday afternoon around three."

Mark thought. In that period of time she could have gotten halfway around the world if she wanted. More than enough time to get to New York. "Listen," he said to Almquist, "if you hear anything let me know, will you?"

"Certainly."

"You can reach me here at my town house in New York or through my office."

Mark gave him his home number, then hung up. Now the pressure was really on. Once she discovered she'd been tricked, Arianna would have probably discounted the danger and barged full speed ahead. That realization made him go cold inside. Meredith had been upset with him, too—so angry that she'd run away, only to be killed. Now Arianna was in the same situation—except that she might be running into the waiting arms of the Mafia. He hadn't meant to hurt either of them, but here he was, on the verge of reliving that same tragic scenario.

ARIANNA GAZED out the window of the bus at the Connecticut countryside. It seemed as if she'd spent a week sitting on airplanes, sitting in various airports and now sitting on the Boston–New York bus. She hadn't slept except for a couple of catnaps, which probably was bad because she wasn't thinking as clearly as she should. But she didn't have much choice if she wanted to get the manuscript to Jerry as fast as she could. To turn an exposé into a real blockbuster, timing was everything. Jerry knew that even better than she. Arianna was determined, though, that he wouldn't be doing it without her.

She also knew there was a tremendous risk involved. The long drive with Kate Throop to Great Falls had given her a chance to think things through. She'd decided that storming into New York would have been stupid. Even if the kidnapping had been a hoax, the break-in at her office wasn't, nor was Corsi's murder.

Arianna knew she'd have to be careful. There was no telling whether or not the Mafia would be watching the airports and train stations, which was why she'd changed planes frequently and was on a bus now.

Once in New York, she figured she could probably check into some little hotel and be safe enough, but she had an even better idea. Mark's town house. It was sitting empty and she had a key. It would be the perfect hideout. Now, if the bus station in the Bronx wasn't being watched, she'd be okay.

But the closer the bus got to New York, the sadder she felt. Here she was, on the eve of the greatest professional triumph of her life, and she wasn't elated. The promise of success didn't offer the joy she'd expected. The truth was, she felt empty and unfulfilled. And she knew why. Mark.

When she first realized that she'd been the victim of a hoax, she'd been angry. How humiliating to think that she'd been taken in so easily. But the more she thought about it, the more she saw that Mark had been trying to protect her.

Of course, she didn't much care for being protected from herself, but in fairness, she had sort of forced him to take extreme measures. Still, his approach was patronizing, and as a matter of principle she couldn't abide the notion that some man—even one she loved—knew what was better for her than she did herself.

That said, she couldn't help being impressed with

how successful Mark had been. Were it not for that chance encounter in the cafeteria with the tattooed man, she'd still be bent over that computer in her underground room, completely oblivious, thinking her superhero had saved her life.

Exactly how Mark had pulled off the charade, and just who or what he truly was, she still didn't know. One thing was certain. He'd been damn clever. Not to mention sexy. As long as she lived, she'd never forget how aroused she felt when he told her he was an operative in a secret government organization.

In a way, she was disappointed that it was a sham. She'd been intrigued with the notion of being a Lindsay girl, but of course, she should have known things like that didn't really happen—except in films. Life wasn't like that.

IT WAS LATE AFTERNOON by the time Arianna's taxi pulled up in front of Mark's town house. She paid the driver and got out. Staring up at the facade of the building that would have been her first home as a married woman, a wave of nostalgia went through her. She hadn't been here since she'd broken their engagement. Maybe it was a mistake to come here now. But she hadn't been able to think of a safer place.

After carrying her bags to the porch, she rang the bell, just to make sure Mark hadn't rented the place to someone. There was no answer so she tried her key. It still worked. She went inside, looked around and saw that the place was empty. Empty, that is, except for all the dreams she and Mark had had for furnishing it.

Arianna forced herself to shake off her nostalgia. As

she stepped into the kitchen, she noticed a phone was still on the wall. She picked up the receiver and was pleased to hear a dial tone. She was in business.

Her initial plan had been to call Jerry at the office first thing in the morning. But it occurred to her now that if she could reach him at home, they might be able to talk in a more leisurely fashion. She dialed Jerry's number.

He answered, surprised to hear her voice. "Arianna, where are you? And do you have the manuscript?"

"Well, I'm so very glad you're fine, too, Jerry."

"Yeah, yeah, you know I love you and your talent both. It's really great to hear from you. I've been worried. And the Sal Corsi thing is getting bigger by the day. So when do I get to see it? Are you in New York?"

"Yes, but I need at least a week more to work on the manuscript."

"Fabulous. I take it the thing holds up..."

"You'll die. It is going to be a huge seller. Corsi nails a lot of big names. And best of all, I've got a line on all his supporting documentation," she said. "Proof of his allegations, apparently."

"Arianna, I *do* love you!"

"It's my project, Jerry."

"It's yours, I agree."

She heaved a sigh of relief. "I'm going to have to lay low while I do this. And I'm going to need some things from you. A computer and a printer would be nice."

"You can have my laptop. And I'll send somebody over to work with you. This is one we'll want on the shelves like day after tomorrow."

"Yes, but I don't need any help, at least not yet. It

would be good if you take care of the legal side, though."

"I've already been looking into it, Arianna."

"I guess the main thing, then, is getting Corsi's documents."

"I can handle that, too," he said. "Where are they?"

She remembered Mark's concern about wiretaps. "I don't think we should discuss that over the phone."

"Okay, why don't we meet, then?" Jerry said. "Where's a convenient place?"

"Do you recall where Mark's town house is?"

He hesitated, then, "Yes, the area, the street."

"Well, the number is 812."

"When should I be there?"

"Let's get it over with," she said.

"I'll grab the laptop and be there as soon as I can."

Arianna hung up, feeling much better knowing things were finally under way. She still was enthusiastic about the project, but for some reason it was feeling more like work than was usual. That surprised her. Maybe Mark was lying more heavily on her mind than she thought.

She glanced around the kitchen, running her hands over the beautiful granite counter. The kitchen designer had promised that the rich chocolate brown of the stone would look wonderful and she was right. Arianna sighed.

As she wandered through the downstairs rooms, she again recalled all their plans for the place. Now what would happen to it? More important, what would happen between her and Mark?

He'd told her he loved her, in spite of the fact that

she'd broken up with him. And she knew she was still attracted to him...more than attracted. She did love him. But she wasn't certain whether or not to trust her feelings. She'd seen so many different sides of Mark in the last few days. Sides she hadn't dreamed existed. That might have said a lot of good things about him, but what did it say about her, especially considering that she had not even suspected that such sides existed?

Well, Madame Wu was right—never judge a book by its cover. God knew, she sure hadn't...not when it came to Mark and not when it came to Corsi's manuscript. Only one thing was certain at this point—she and Mark had a lot of talking to do. Even if there was no Alpha, no 007, no James Bond or Superman, she would have to deal with Clark Kent. Come to think of it, that wasn't so bad. In fact, he had to be pretty darn special to have come up with that plan and pulled it off. That took a super man, or at least a super clever man.

As she returned to the barren front room, she heard the sound of a key in the front door. She thought of the manuscript, recalled all the things it said the Mafia did when someone thwarted them, and her heart stopped. Unable to move, she watched with horror as the door swung open, admitting the fading light of dusk into the room. But then she saw Mark! Her eyes rounded with surprise. He was in running shoes, shorts and a T-shirt. He was sweating heavily. She couldn't believe it.

"Arianna," he said when he saw her. "What are you

doing here?" He flipped on the light switch just inside the door. The disbelief on his face mirrored her own.

It took her a moment to gather her wits. "I escaped," she finally said. "But what are *you* doing here, Mark?"

"The last time I checked, my name was on the deed," he said, closing the door. "I've been out for a run, trying to burn off some pent-up energy."

"Secret mission over, or just the charade?"

"They told me you'd left, that you knew everything." Mark smiled weakly. "Desperate situations called for desperate measures."

Arianna hadn't been sure how she'd react when she saw him. Most of her anger had already faded, but seeing him, so disarming-looking in his workout clothes, a contrite expression on his face, her heart softened. But she wasn't going to signal her forgiveness too quickly. He had some explaining to do.

"Speaking of which, I would like a few answers, 007," she told him. "I think I've figured out some of it, but not all." Her eyes narrowed. "That kidnapping was faked, wasn't it? The gangsters were Consolidated employees."

"That's right."

"And the watch. There wasn't any homing beacon in it, was there?"

He shook his head. "Nope, it's the watch I've had forever."

"Mark," she said, putting her hands on her hips. "Aren't you just a little embarrassed? I mean, an investment banker pretending he's James Bond?"

He walked toward her. "Ah, but you enjoyed the game, too, didn't you, Arianna?"

"I suppose I did," she said, her heart picking up its beat.

"But you're still angry?"

"I was at first."

Mark stopped in front of her. "How about now?"

She gazed into his eyes, expecting to see the old Mark. But the man she saw seemed to be the one she'd made love with in a Colorado chalet and a Montana missile site, the one who'd lured her and frustrated her, teased and confounded her—unless that was wishful thinking on her part. "I guess I'm wondering if you were really that clever, or if I was that stupid."

"Oh, I was clever. Definitely."

"Too clever for your own good," she said, giving him a look. "How did you arrange all that, anyway? Helicopters and paramilitary troops and gunfights. Do you know somebody in Hollywood or what?"

He grinned. "Ah, now that you've admitted you liked it, you want to know all my secrets, is that it?"

She arched an eyebrow. "I think the least you can do is tell me the truth."

Mark glanced around the room. "Too bad this place is so empty. I'm tired and I'd like to sit down." He sighed. "Oh, I know, the stairs."

They went to the staircase and Mark dropped onto a step. Arianna sat beside him. She was feeling conciliatory, but she still wasn't ready to let him off the hook. Besides, she really did wonder how he'd done it.

"When we were on our way to Vail, and I realized I wasn't going to be able to talk you out of coming back to New York," he began, "I decided to call in some old markers. Those first few days when I left the chalet, I was setting everything up."

"Hiring people to stage the big drama, you mean?"

"I didn't need to hire anybody, sweetpea. I just asked my friends at Alpha for help."

"Come on, Mark. The game's over. There's no Alpha."

"Oh, but there is. I assure you, it's quite real."

"Are you trying to tell me you really are a secret agent?" she asked with disbelief.

"In a way. I dramatized a bit, but Alpha does all the things I told you they did. And I have worked with them—though more as an outsider."

"Well, you can't stop there. I want to hear it all."

Mark rubbed his jaw, as if he was considering his words carefully. "About three years ago Lindsay and Soames was approached by some people at Alpha. Until then, we'd never even heard of the organization. They really are top-secret.

"Anyway, Alpha had a company in South America that they wanted financed for political reasons. It wasn't the sort of investment that made a lot of sense financially, but Alpha needed our help, and in any case, we weren't being asked to put up our investor's money. The funds were to come from another source. So we did it.

"Several times since then I've cooperated with Alpha, providing either a source of information, as was the case on a project in Russia, or acting as a conduit for capital. The point is, Alpha was indebted to me. And I needed them to do me a favor."

"It must have been a pretty big favor, Mark. That was no small operation."

"True. And it took some effort to set up. That time I was gone all day from the chalet, I met with Jones and we planned the whole scheme. I even rehearsed the karate kick."

"My God," she said, incredulous. "I guess I am impressed, after all."

"I sort of like it that we didn't have to actually kill anybody," he said, tongue in cheek.

"So Consolidated is an Alpha front, after all?"

"No, Consolidated was formed with the discreet help of the U.S. and Japanese governments. Alpha was instrumental in the project, and Jones knew a number of the key people at Consolidated, including George Almquist, the Montana plant manager. Almquist made the company's executive aircraft available and offered the use of the facility. The paramilitary troops were actually from the local search and rescue team in Colorado. They received a generous donation for their time and effort. Jones rented the helicopters from a commercial company."

Arianna nodded. "And I suppose that was catsup on those bodies?"

"Red paint."

"Mark," she said, jabbing him with her elbow, "I could just kill you. I had nightmares about people being shot and killed."

"Well, I had nightmares about *you* being shot and killed. So I'd say we're even."

Arianna looked into his eyes, realizing that although

the whole thing had been a hoax, Mark wasn't really a phony. "In a way, you *are* a spy, aren't you?" she said.

"Let's say fellow traveler."

"You're sort of a blend of the Mark I used to know, and the Mark I saw in Vail and Montana. Aren't you?"

"That's right. When I told you about my conversation with Zara, and my resolve to be true to myself, I was being totally honest." He took her hand. "If I'd done that from the first, I don't think you'd have ever felt suffocated. It was a huge mistake."

Arianna looked into his eyes. "I haven't been without blame. I didn't appreciate you as I should have because I was too wrapped up in my career. I didn't communicate my feelings, either."

"The trick was to be myself and let the chips fall where they may."

Arianna gave him a telling look. "Not *all* the chips. You still weren't willing to let me come back to New York."

"No, and I agonized over it, believe me. I didn't want to be overly protective, yet I knew you weren't paying sufficient heed to the danger. Finally I decided your life was a hell of a lot more important than anything else. If I had to lie and cheat, I would lie and cheat. In a way, by kidnapping you, I was really setting you free."

Arianna glanced down at his hand that was intertwined in hers, feeling a tremendous warmth and tenderness. She could tell he meant exactly what he was saying. Ironically, it made her want to throw her arms around his neck. "I loved you for it, too, Mark," she said. "And I want you to know that I've been humbled by this experience."

Mark took her chin in his hand. "God, you aren't going to go soft on me, are you, sweetpea?"

"Of course not. I wouldn't go *that* far."

He laughed. "Assuming we continue seeing each other, I can see that it's going to be a battle every step of the way."

"You know why that is, Mark?"

"Why?"

"I like the idea of being a Lindsay girl, but I don't like the idea of being one of many. Or even one of a few. I want to be it, the one and only."

"Hmm," he said, stroking his chin, "that's going to be a problem."

She blinked. "What do you mean?"

"Alpha's not shy about asking for sacrifices. A good agent is expected to go to the limit and beyond. Whatever it takes to get the job done, including cavorting with beautiful women."

"Maybe we need to rethink this Alpha business," she said, her eyes narrowing.

Grinning, Mark took her face in his hands and kissed her. Arianna was beginning to think that going back into hiding might not be such a bad idea, when she heard a car door slam out front.

"Oh," she said.

"What's the matter?"

"That's probably Jerry."

"Jerry?"

"Yes, before you got back I called him and told him I was here. We were going to talk about the book."

Mark rolled his eyes. "I don't suppose there's any chance you'll just hand the damn thing over and tell him to take it."

"I'm tempted, to be honest."

"Well, handle it as you see fit. I'm going upstairs to grab a shower."

She gave him a quick kiss. "Let me take you to dinner tonight, Mark."

"I'll think about it," he said with a quirky smile.

She gave him another jab and Mark, laughing, got to his feet and trotted up the stairs. The doorbell rang and Arianna went to greet her boss. Her moment of triumph was upon her, but what she was really looking forward to was dinner with the man she loved.

14

ARIANNA PULLED the door open. Jerry stood there, a laptop computer in his arms and his eyes as round as baseballs. He was forty, slender and had a full head of prematurely white hair. At the moment he looked terrified, like the proverbial deer in the headlights of an oncoming truck.

"Jerry, what's wrong?"

The words had barely passed her lips before two men appeared from the shadows, taking Jerry by the arms and shoving their way into the room. Out of nowhere two more men appeared, following Jerry and the first two in the door.

"What's going on?" she demanded. "Who are you?"

The man closest to her gave her a shove backward to show he meant business. "Shut your mouth," he said.

"What *is* this?" she insisted.

"I said shut up, lady, and I mean it."

Arianna stood facing four rough-looking men and poor Jerry, whose expression was frozen in terror, his shoulders rounded and hunched, his demeanor indicating he expected to be whacked over the head at any moment. The man who'd shoved her took her by the arm. He was short and stout, his skin bad, his black oily hair combed perfectly. He wore a dark blue pin-striped suit and smelled of garlic and tobacco.

"You got the book?" he said.

"I beg your pardon?"

"The book, dammit, Corsi's book. Where is it?"

Jerry groaned. "I d-didn't know," he stammered. "They jumped me as soon as I stepped out of the taxi, Arianna. I really—"

"Shut that twit up!" the first man growled at his companions.

A big guy with a crewcut and a suit coat that hung on him like a tent hit Jerry on the shoulder, nearly making him drop the computer. The other two fanned around the room. The whole bunch of them looked as if they'd come right out of central casting. Too good to be true. It was then that she realized it *was* too good to be true.

"Oh," she said, smiling. "I see. We're playing gangster again."

The men seemed completely baffled when she laughed and went to the foot of the stairs.

"Very funny, Mark!" she called up to him. "Fool me once, shame on you. Fool me twice, shame on me!" Then she looked at the men, all of whom appeared thoroughly perplexed. "You guys are better than the last bunch, I'll say that. You really look the part."

"What's with the broad?" the one with the crewcut said.

"I don't know," the first man replied. He walked over to where Arianna stood, mirthful. "You got somebody upstairs, or you just nuts, lady?"

"*You* spend a lot of time at the movies," she said. "You have a good ear for dialogue."

He shook his head. "We got a nutcase, all right, boys. Just what we need."

Arianna chuckled. Then, stepping past her inquisitor, she went over to Jerry. "It's a gag," she said. "Mark hired them, the devil."

"She ain't nuts, Ernie," the man with the crewcut said. "She needs to be slapped upside the head, that's all."

"Arianna," Jerry said under his breath, his tone desperate. "Can't you see they're serious? What's wrong with you?"

"Good question," Ernie said, stepping over and taking her arm again. He jerked her around.

"Somebody upstairs or not?"

"Only James Bond."

Ernie slapped her face, startling her. "Hey!"

He ignored her, turning to the other two men. "Al, you and Carlo take a look." Then Ernie looked her dead in the eye, his garlic breath washing over her. "All right, sister, the book. I want it *now*."

"For God's sake, Arianna," Jerry said, "give him the damn thing."

"Now there's a smart man," Ernie said. "Listen to him."

Arianna couldn't figure out why they were persisting. She'd already told them she was on to them. Surely Mark wouldn't have told them to take it over the top. "Mark?" she called, her voice shaking a little. Doubt was beginning to set in.

Then she heard scuffling upstairs and a shout. Lord, she said to herself, this couldn't be for real, could it?

She looked over at her bags, where she'd stuffed the manuscript. Ernie noticed.

"The book in the suitcase, sweetheart?"

There was a commotion at the top of the stairs and the two men who'd gone up reappeared with Mark between them. He was in a bathrobe.

"Look what we found, Ern," one said.

As the trio reached the bottom of the stairs, Arianna saw the distraught look on Mark's face. An icy chill ran through her blood. It couldn't be.

"Mark, if this is a joke, it's time to stop and laugh about it," she said.

He shook his head. "It's no joke."

"It's *not?*" Her stomach dropped so hard, she felt sick.

"All right," Ernie said, "this is getting old. Carlo, bring those suitcases over here. The broad is going to hand over the book so we can get our butts out of here."

Arianna peered desperately into Mark's eyes. He'd been a pretty good actor last time around, but was he topping himself, or was this really the Mafia? "Time to push that little button," she said, catching his eye.

"There's no Jones this time," he said glumly.

"Mark?" She was uncertain. She couldn't bear the thought of being made the fool twice. On the other hand, the corner of her mouth was throbbing from that slap. "Oh, God," she muttered.

The suitcases were set at her feet.

"Open them," Ernie ordered. "And be quick about it."

Arianna bent down and opened the case that contained the manuscript. Pulling it out, she handed it to the man.

"This it?"

"That's the whole thing," she replied.

"Seems like our friend Sal had some documents that went with this thing," Ernie said. "You got 'em?"

"No," she replied.

"But you know where they are, right?"

She hesitated. "No."

"That no sounded like yes to me, sweetheart. Give! And make it snappy."

"I don't have it," she said firmly. "Corsi gave me a note saying he had supporting documentation, and that he could provide it if necessary. He obviously didn't expect you to kill him before he could hand it over." She was whistling in the dark and hoped to God it didn't show.

"Know what?" Ernie said. "The only thing worse than an ugly broad is a broad with a mouth. Gonzo," he said, turning to the hulk with the crewcut, "put your piece in Perry White's ear. Al, you do the boy-friend."

To Arianna's utter horror, the two men stuck guns against the heads of Jerry and Mark. Jerry looked as though he was about to pee in his pants. Mark was grim. Arianna began shaking.

"This is where we play 'you-pick-who-gets-it,'" Ernie said. "One of the boys here is going to pull the trig-ger. Then I count to five. If you haven't told me where the papers are by that time, then the second guy goes down. That's the sad part. It's really a lot of fun."

"You wouldn't," she said, aghast.

"I'll let you pick," he said. "Boss or boyfriend first?"

"Arianna," Jerry whined, "for God's sakes!"

"If you don't pick," Ernie said, "I will." He peered back and forth between the two men.

"Arianna!" Jerry shouted.

"Everybody ready?" Ernie said, grinning. "Time to see how much the broad cares."

"The documents are in a mail drop in Brooklyn," she snapped. "The address is on a slip of paper in my purse."

"Ah, a woman with brains," Ernie said. "Now let's see if you're truthful, too. Carlo, get the purse."

The man brought it to Arianna. She removed the slip of paper and handed it over. Ernie examined it. "Perfect." He reached out and patted her cheek like a benevolent grandfather. "Boys," he said, "time to take a powder."

The men had no sooner holstered their guns when the front door flew open and another group of men came charging in, guns drawn. "FBI!" they shouted. "Everybody freeze!"

The gangsters, Jerry, Mark and Arianna stood stunned as the new arrivals streamed into the room. Grabbing Ernie and his men, they shoved them against the wall, disarmed them and then put them in cuffs. Arianna turned to Mark, who looked equally bewildered and elated.

"Arianna," Jerry said, coming up to them, "if you'd let them shoot me, I'd have fired you, I swear I would have."

"Getting your job did cross my mind," she teased. "But I decided I'd rather get it with your help."

One of the supposed FBI agents walked up to Mark. "Mr. Lindsay," he said, "we meet again."

"Hello, Agent Murphy," he said. "Nice timing." He glanced over at Arianna and gave her a wink.

"Mark Lindsay," she said, "did you get me again?"

Murphy stepped over to her. "Miss Hamilton, I presume."

She glared at him, her eyes narrow. "So, you're FBI, huh?"

"Yes, ma'am. Hap Murphy, agent in charge of the New York office."

"I don't suppose you have a badge, Agent Murphy."

"Yes, ma'am, I do."

He reached into his coat pocket and produced a leather case, which he flipped open. Arianna examined it closely. It said Federal Bureau of Investigation, and had Murphy's name on it. She shook her head in disbelief.

"You're for real?"

"As real as the law allows, Miss Hamilton."

She put her hands to her mouth. "And these guys are really in the Mafia?"

Murphy looked over at the handcuffed men, all under the guard of agents. "That's Ernie 'the Salami' Fapolli. We've been on his tail since Corsi went down at JFK. He's been watching Mr. Salter and we've been watching him. Since this morning we've been hanging around Mr. Lindsay's place, as well. It started getting interesting when everybody showed up here."

"My God," Jerry said. "I walked right into a trap."

"I think everybody's here for the same reason,"

Murphy said, glancing at the manuscript pages scattered on the floor. "That, I assume, is Corsi's book."

Arianna and Jerry exchanged glances.

"I'm going to have to take it as evidence," Murphy said. He signaled one of the other agents to pick up the manuscript.

"But you're going to let us make photocopies first, right?" Jerry said.

"Afraid not, Mr. Salter."

"But what harm will that do?"

"We're going to be conducting a very delicate criminal prosecution and we can't jeopardize it. In fact, I'm going to have to ask if you've already made copies."

Arianna sighed. "Yes. On some disks in my purse."

"Would you please get them for me, Miss Hamilton?"

She got the disks she'd made in Montana and handed them to Agent Murphy.

"Thank you," he said. "Is this it?"

"Yes."

"And now, the most critical item of all. The supporting documentation."

Arianna went to where Ernie had dropped the slip of paper on the floor when the FBI had charged in. She picked it up and handed it to Murphy. "I'm giving you what could have made my career, I hope you realize that," she said.

"The criminal justice system exists for the protection of all of us," Murphy replied.

"Isn't there a way we can have our cake and let you eat it, too?" Jerry asked.

Murphy shook his head. "I'm afraid not. At least not until after the trial and appeals have run their course."

"That'll be too late."

"I'm sorry." Murphy managed to look regretful. "Now, if you folks will excuse me, please. All right," he said to his associates. "Let's get these boys out of here."

Arianna, Mark and Jerry watched as the FBI herded the gangsters out the front door. The manuscript, the disks and the address of the mail drop went with them. The closing door echoed through the empty town house.

"Well," Arianna said wistfully, "it was fun while it lasted."

"I thought for a while you were going to get us all killed," Jerry said, handing her the laptop computer.

She looked at Mark. "I was sure you'd set the whole thing up."

"No, I was leaning toward hiring a bunch of Russian mercenaries to do the job, but the real bad guys beat me to the punch."

"Nice to know you were still thinking of my welfare," she said, taking his arm.

Mark kissed her temple. "For a while there, I was afraid reality was going to overtake fiction."

"Seems to me it did," Jerry moaned. "Why did you have to give them the disks, too, Arianna? They never would have known."

"Until the book showed up on the stands."

"We've got good lawyers."

She peered up into Mark's eyes, thinking of the dinner she owed him, the evening she wanted to spend with him. "Maybe I'm too honest, Jerry," she said. "Maybe I should just stick with movie stars and politicians and society figures."

"Maybe we should talk about that," Jerry said, looking at his watch. "Well, I've blown a Sunday and all I've got to show for it is an ulcer. I'm going home and drinking a bottle of Scotch. Will I see you in the office tomorrow, Arianna?"

"I need a couple of days off, Jerry."

"You can have one. See you Tuesday morning." With that he headed toward the door. "Oh, nice seeing you, Mark," he said over his shoulder. "Like your town house." He was gone.

Arianna turned to Mark and took his hands. "I'm at a loss for words," she said. "The best rides in Disneyland don't compare with an hour with you."

He ran a finger down her cheek. "Which hour are you referring to?"

She smiled, turning red with embarrassment. "You don't have a bed upstairs by any chance."

"No, but I have a futon."

She pressed his fingers to her cheek. "That'll do."

"For what?"

"The interrogation I'm putting you through after I take you to dinner."

"You know all my secrets, sweetpea. There's nothing left."

She gazed into his eyes for a long time. "You know what? I think I'm glad it ended this way."

"Why's that?"

"I wasn't meant to be the sensation of the publishing industry."

"Hey, that's not the Arianna Hamilton I know and love," he said, cupping her face.

"You'd rather I be chasing a book at the risk of life and limb?"

Mark took her by the shoulders. "Tell me the truth, if I could produce a copy of that manuscript, you'd grab it in a New York minute, wouldn't you?"

"But you can't. The only copy was on those disks and the FBI took them."

Mark shook his head. "You aren't thinking like a spy. How did you get those copies onto the disks?"

"From that computer you got for me in Montana."

"Right. They came off the hard drive, *n'est-ce pas?*"

"That's right!" she said, her mouth dropping open. "I forgot all about that! The scanned copy is on that computer in my room at the missile site!"

"Bingo."

"Unless it's been erased or Consolidated won't let me have it."

"True."

"But Alpha owes you, doesn't it, Mark? Couldn't you give them a call and have them make another copy off the hard drive and send it to us."

"There's one little problem," he said. "Alpha doesn't owe me anything now. In fact, I owe them."

She frowned. "What does that mean?"

"If I want something from them, I'm going to have to agree to take on more assignments. When they have a need, I'll have to accommodate them."

"In other words, we might be in bed some night and the phone will ring and you'll have to run off for a secret rendezvous with some shapely blond Swedish secret agent."

"Precisely."

"And since you'll be sworn to secrecy, I'll never know what's real and not real, when you're being honest and when you're lying for the sake of your country."

"Afraid so."

Arianna bit her lip. "That's sort of like making me decide which kid to sacrifice to the wolf."

"Life can be difficult," he said. "The price of fame is eternal uncertainty."

She rubbed her chin.

"So, what's it's going to be, Arianna?" he asked. "Shall I call George Almquist and have him send me a disk with a copy of the Corsi book, or do you want to know where I *really* am every night?"

Her eyes narrowed. "You're a nice guy, Mark, but you truly are a bastard."

He laughed. "You can always pick...like Ernie said."

She shook her head. "You're loving this, aren't you?"

"Hey, I'm just curious what you're going to do."

Arianna gave him a coy look. "I'll let you know later. After I have dinner and check out that futon."

"Sounds like you're putting the pressure on me to perform," he said.

"For an old hand like you, it ought to be a piece of cake."

Mark gave her a wry grin. "I already know what you're going to do, Arianna."

"Oh?"

"James Bond was never wrong, was he?"

"James Bond never settled for one woman," she said.

He took her face in his hands. "Yeah. But James Bond never tangled with you."

F O R T U N E **C O O K I E**

The romance continues in four spin-off books.

Discover what destiny has in store when
Lina, Arianna, Briana and Molly crack open
their fortune cookies!

PAIN CAN BE THE MIDWIFE OF JOY

THIS CHILD IS MINE
Janice Kaiser
Superromance #761
October 1997

NEVER JUDGE A BOOK BY ITS COVER

DOUBLE TAKE
Janice Kaiser
Temptation #659
November 1997

DISCOVER YOUR DREAMS AND DISCOVER YOURSELF

THE DREAM WEDDING
M.J. Rodgers
Intrigue #445
December 1997

FOLLOW YOUR DREAM

JOE'S GIRL
Margaret St. George
American Romance #710
January 1998

Available wherever Harlequin books are sold.

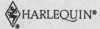
HARLEQUIN®

Every month there's another title from one
of your favorite authors!

October 1997
Romeo in the Rain by Kasey Michaels
When Courtney Blackmun's daughter brought home Mr. Tall,
Dark and Handsome, Courtney wanted to send the young
matchmaker to her room! Of course, that meant the single
New Jersey mom would be left alone with the irresistibly
attractive Adam Richardson....

November 1997
Intrusive Man by Lass Small
Indiana's Hannah Calhoun had enough on her hands taking
care of her young son, and the last thing she needed was a
man complicating things—especially Max Simmons, the
gorgeous cop who had eased himself right into her little boy's
heart...and was making his way into hers.

December 1997
Crazy Like a Fox by Anne Stuart
Moving in with her deceased husband's—*eccentric*—family
in Louisiana meant a whole new life for Margaret Jaffrey and
her nine-year-old daughter. But the beautiful young widow
soon finds herself seduced by the slower pace and the much-
too-attractive cousin-in-law, Peter Andrew Jaffrey....

**BORN IN THE USA: Love, marriage—
and the pursuit of family!**

Available at your favorite retail outlet!

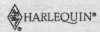 

DEBBIE MACOMBER

invites you to the

HEART OF TEXAS

Join Debbie Macomber as she brings you the lives
and loves of the folks in the ranching community
of Promise, Texas.

If you loved Midnight Sons—don't miss
Heart of Texas! A brand-new six-book series
from Debbie Macomber.

Available in February 1998
at your favorite retail store.

Heart of Texas by Debbie Macomber

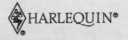
HARLEQUIN®

HPHRT1

Look what Santa brought!

CHRISTMAS DELIVERY

Capture the holiday spirit with these three
heartwarming stories of moms, dads,
babies and mistletoe. *Christmas Delivery*
is the perfect stocking stuffer featuring three
of your favorite authors:

A CHRISTMAS MARRIAGE by Dallas Schulze
DEAR SANTA by Margaret St. George
THREE WAIFS AND A DADDY by Margot Dalton

**There's always room for one more—
especially at Christmas!**

Available wherever Harlequin and Silhouette
books are sold.

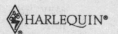 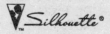